Zero Degrees of Separation

SANDRA HATFIELD

D1295399

Zero Degrees of Separation
by Sandra Hatfield

Copyright © 2007 by Sandra Hatfield

ISBN 0-96-38490-3-4

All rights reserved. No part of this book may be used or reproduced in
any manner whatsoever without written permission except in a case of
brief quotations embodied in critical articles and reviews.

This is a work of fiction. Names, characters, places, and incidents
wither are the product of the author's imagination or are used
fictitiously, and any resemblance to actual persons, living or dead,
business establishments, events, or locales is entirely coincidental.
The publisher does not have any control over and does not assume any
responsibility for author or third-party websites or their content.

Published by:
Harmony Grove Marketing
2870 Highway 326
Commerce, GA 30530

First Quality Paperback Edition 2008

Edited by Ronnie Mound Foster, ronnierennae@hughes.net

Interior layout and design: Jennifer Foster

Cover Design: Jennifer Foster, designmaven@mac.com

Printed and bound in the United States of America.

DEDICATION

To my best friend, my soul mate, my loving husband..
A love that is never-ending and ever-lasting, eternally.
We are still learning from each other.

To my Family waiting for me.

ACKNOWLEDGMENTS

A heartfelt thanks and sincere appreciation to Kathryn and Dannion Brinkley, Dr. Ed Shotts, my dear friend and Editor, Ronnie Foster, and daughter Jennifer Foster for her beautiful cover design and her publishing knowledge, without whose assistance and support, you would not be reading this book.

I would also like to give special recognition to all those wonderful people facing end-of-life whom I have known and have yet to know, who are still with us and who have gone on, and are the most beautiful and courageous people in the world. They know things we do not yet know and have been some of my greatest teachers.

Dear Reader,

This book was written as a novel and there are no claims to be factual, but was intended as a "doorway to possibility." There were many portions of this book in which I was 'guided' to write. Therefore, if any part of this story rings true for you, or if it has alleviated or lessened any fears you may have about death and dying, then this book has served its purpose.

With "Undying" Love,

Sandra Hatfield

ONE AND INDESTRUCTIBLE

Each one of us, however, must be prepared for the day
when our loved ones will leave us in what the world
calls death.
But this is not really separation because what we
love of each other is not the body: It is the
consciousness. If God has breathed into us the life of
God, then the life of God is the life of man, and we can
never be separated from our life, not even in death
because "I and my Father are one": I and my life are
one, I and my love are one, one and indestructible.

Joel S. Goldsmith "Consciousness Is What I Am"

FOREWARD
By Dannion Brinkley

For the past 30 years I have been a hospice volunteer and have been at the bedside of 369 people taking their last breath. I have spent time with 1,800 people during their final days, and have dedicated more than 26,000 hours of bedside service.

This all came about as a result of being struck by lightening in 1975 and being pronounced clinically dead for 28 minutes. I spent two years convalescing from that incident, and because of the damage done to my body, had two more near-death experiences over the next twenty-two years. From these experiences, the needs of the dying and those caring for them, became very clear to me.

I co-founded THE TWILIGHT BRIGADE, *Compassion in Action*, in 1997. We are a non-profit volunteer, end-of-life care organization, training people to become transition specialists across the United States. These dedicated volunteers bring comfort to the dying and assist in empowering those they leave behind. I am so very proud of those who have chosen to take the time and effort to write from their hearts, to share the insights that have been gained from their service.

Zero Degrees of Separation was written by Sandy, one of our National Trainers and a hospice volunteer, in an effort to alleviate pain and suffering due to fears associated with the dying process. Much of the information obtained for her book has come from her connection with her Angels and is presented with the hope that it will help people prepare for their own transition and that of their loved ones, by introducing possibilities of that magnificent shift from the earth realm to "home." As someone who has been on the other side three times, I can say that even though this book is a work of fiction, there's a lot of truth to be found here.

With purpose,
Dannion Brinkley

Zero Degrees of Separation

Christina awoke to find seven beautiful people standing around her. Although she felt she knew, or had known them, she was a little foggy-headed and definitely not clear as to where she was or how she got there. Wherever *there* was.

The individual standing at her right shoulder said, "We are all here to help you. Just relax and don't be afraid." At that moment she realized she had not heard the words or seen them spoken, but rather "felt" them instead.

As the fog was just beginning to lift, it seemed it brought forth a minimum of 100 questions. Naturally, the first regarded Christina's whereabouts; and furthermore, the mode of transportation enabling her to reach this place with all memory of it wiped completely from her mind. "Why can't I remember?" She asked herself silently.

"Who are you and where am I?" Christine asked in a mild state of panic. Somewhere deep in the back of her mind she instinctively knew she had no reason to be afraid. Surely just by observing these people and the calm, reassuring looks on their faces told her they were not the enemy.

In answer to her questions before she could even verbalize them, one of the women said, "We just helped you over and you have been resting."

Feeling a discomfort she had no explanation for Christina asked "Is that like 'eating over' or 'sleeping over?' Is that what you mean? I don't remember being invited anywhere and at my age, I can't imagine accepting any such invitation. Who invited me?"

"Too many questions, too fast. Let's take this slowly and we will eventually answer them all," said the beautiful blonde woman.

It struck Christina they all looked young, perhaps 25 to 30 years of age, but their eyes belied that, full of wisdom and maturity. She had always heard the eyes were the window to the soul and the phrase "Wisdom of the Ages" came to her as she looked into their faces.

"Who are these people?" she thought to herself and the dark-haired woman answered, "We will answer that, and more, in due time." This was unnerving, unsettling and certainly unfair.

Christina sat up on the edge of the bed and said, "Let's get started. Prove to me I'm not crazy or dreaming or suffering from brain damage. Who *are* you people?"

The man at her shoulder acted as spokesperson and introduced himself as Bruce. He was very tall with white shoulder-length hair, hazel eyes with beautiful features and an air of authority with a gentleness that had an instant calming effect. He then introduced each of the others.

"This is Lily," he said turning to his right and reaching out and touching the shoulder of a stunning blonde with blue eyes. She was not only powerfully beautiful and very tall for a woman, but she was imbued with the same calmness about her.

Ellen was standing next to her, radiant with silky-soft black hair and matching eyes and a smile that went forever. She was linking arms with James, almost twin-like in appearance to Ellen, with penetrating eyes that housed enormous kindness.

The next young man was Arthur, not nearly as tall as the others and a bit rounder, but still in good form. His red hair and freckles gave him an affable and somewhat whimsical appearance.

"Likable fellow," Christina thought, at which he smiled and winked. She immediately made a mental note to stop doing that or to make sure everything she thought about someone else was in good taste.

The last two were women, Felicia and Sarah. Felicia had long wavy brown hair and brilliant blue eyes, crystal in quality. Sarah, another redhead with skin like ivory and eyes so green they made you think of velvet or the mossy banks of a clear stream. Christina felt an instant rapport with Felicia and Sarah, not that she didn't feel some sort of kinship with the others; but these two women were special to her. Although what their relationship to her was, at this moment she did not know. Yet.

Realizing she appeared overwhelmed and looked confused, Bruce asked, "What is the last thing you remember before finding yourself here?"

Christina thought for a moment, the simple act producing something that likens that of a headache, but with no pain associated. "Strange sensation," she thought. This was only the first of many more to come.

"The last thing I remember," she said as she winced, "was lying in a hospital bed... not this one... and being in a lot of pain. Most of all, I remember the grief at the thought of leaving my family soon.

"My God! My family! Where are they? Are they here? How come the pain has gone?" She suddenly realized she had never felt better in her life. "My husband Bill and my daughters Anne and Karen...where are they?"

Bruce lightly placed his hand on Christina's forehead, sending a mild shock wave of comfort all the way to her toes, eliminating all her immediate concerns. Bruce said, "We do not want you becoming agitated again and as I said, all your questions will be answered. You are in good hands. Your husband and children are fine and well, as you are. However, they are not here. It is simply a matter of change. You have left the pain behind, at your own choice. Now, what is the next thing you remember?"

CHAPTER 2

Christina found herself back in the hospital room, not exactly experiencing that unbelievable pain but full of the memory of it. She was gripping her husband's hand and looking at her daughters thinking, "How beautiful they are. Both girls in their twenties and married, happily, thank heaven! At least I know they will be taken care of and happy. I no longer need to worry about them when I leave.

"But Bill, what will happen to him? We have been happily married for 26 years, and we have shared so much together. I can't leave him! I could never imagine my life without him and I know he feels the same way." Inwardly Christina knew the decision had already been made.

Christina and Bill had been high school sweethearts. It was one of those rare relationships that weathered many storms and became stronger for it. She fell for him the moment she laid eyes on him. He was tall with somewhat unruly black hair, and had an ivy-league look to him no matter how he dressed. Since Christina was tall herself, she was extremely comfortable with Bill's height. He had a decent build, but not because he worked out, he was just blessed with it. Unlike Christina, he never had to worry about what he ate. He carried himself with an air of self-confidence, which appealed to her. She always made it a point to smile her biggest and best smile when he looked at her. Her mother had taught her that it sometimes helped if you looked at him out of the corner of your eye while smiling, too. She tried it all. She had made up her mind that he was the man for her.

Finally the big moment arrived when the school had a "turn-around" dance where the girls got to ask the boys and it was acceptable. She called him after school and, without a second's hesitation, he accepted her invitation. She was not only the happiest girl at the dance, but the proudest. Bill was a great dancer, he was tall, he was charming, he had a great sense of humor, and he was a gentleman. She would always feel this way about him. From that moment on, both their names rolled off people's tongues as one name. They were always together. You rarely saw one without the other. By current-day standards they were truly a couple "out of time."

Bill was quite taken with Christina from the minute he met her during his senior year in high school. She was nothing like his mental image of the one he would spend his life with, but better. He first saw her walking down the school corridor with some of her friends, each of which paled by comparison. Christina stood out from the rest wherever she went and whomever she was with. She was tall and slender with a small frame. Not overly endowed, but well proportioned with long legs. She had strawberry blonde hair just past shoulder length that had hint of a curl to it. This gave it the appearance of always just having been brushed. Her face, with its slightly freckled nose, always had a smile on it for everyone she met. She laughed easily and life enjoyed her! He knew instantly this was the woman he was going to marry...without question. Now, to somehow let her know this. As soon as he finds a way to meet her, of course.

Bill forgot who and where he was as he stood in that hallway staring at Christina. Naturally this evoked a lot of unnecessary comments from his buddies walking with him to their chemistry class. They grabbed his arms and nearly dragged him to the classroom while laughing at their lovesick friend. They reached their stations in the classroom and when Bill looked up he saw Christina two aisles away, facing him. She smiled that contagious smile at him and he felt himself grow weak. He was barely able to raise his arm and manage a feeble wave. He felt he must look like the Queen of England waving from her carriage. "Stupid! Dumb! Great show! You must have made a spectacular impression on her with your overwhelming self-confidence and forcefulness!" he mumbled to himself, knowing any chance with her was as strong as his wave.

After class, Christina was the one to walk up and say, "Hi!"

Once again Bill's knees turned to water, but he managed his biggest smile and brilliantly said, "Hi!"

Christina laughed one of her easy laughs and introduced herself. This put him somewhat at ease so, over the lump in his throat, Bill introduced himself to the woman of his future. The worst of it was over and the best was yet to come.

Bill figured she was brighter than average, even though she didn't really overtax herself in her classes. She did just enough to get through, being more interested in living life and having fun. Later he came to find out that brighter-than-average was an understatement. She excelled in music and after completing her studies she became a grade school music teacher.

They grew together instead of away from each other with similar interests yet respect for each other's privacy. They did almost everything together, not out of duty, but because it was what they wanted. They truly enjoyed each other's company as friends and lovers.

Christina's illness had been a crushing blow to them both. They had raised their children, who were now off starting their own married lives. For the first time Bill and Christina had the spare time to devote to one another and to do the things they had only dreamed about until now. They had worked hard and saved enough money for a well-planned, long-awaited trip to Europe. They played like a couple of kids and were mistaken for newlyweds on their honeymoon. An assumption they never bothered to correct. It was the vacation of a lifetime.

Two months after their return home Christina was diagnosed with cancer. They both vowed they were going to "lick this thing together." However, the pains continued to increase after the surgery to remove the tumor, indicating the cancer had spread. The misery of chemotherapy, the irritability and resultant hair loss still did nothing to dampen the love Bill and Christina had for each other. Instead Bill spent more time with Christina even taking days off work to be with her. In spite of her extreme weight loss, pale color and weakness, when Bill looked at her he still saw that beautiful strawberry blonde in high school. Even though she was forty-six years old, in his eyes she was a senior in chemistry class, smiling at him.

On the good days they would take long walks together along the river only a few blocks from their home. It was particularly enjoyable in the Fall. The beautifully colored leaves would crunch under their feet and be the only sound during their quiet times. It was unnecessary to talk, and they would hold hands for the comfort they each needed.

To Bill's mind, Christina was the perfect person for him. He could not have custom ordered anyone to suit him more. He loved her mind and the way she could jump from subject to subject and not lose the thread weaving the thoughts together. She made him laugh, and made him feel good about everything, including himself. She had a positive approach to life in general, which he needed to keep him from drowning in his self-made reality. He thought of himself as looking at things realistically, but Christina teased him saying it was just negativity. She was a perfect balance for him. What they had was good.

They often knew what each other was thinking and many times would finish sentences for each other. It was the kind of relationship most people only dream about and never have the opportunity to experience. They both knew this to be true, which made them appreciate and cherish what they had even more.

Returning from her beautiful memories, Christina said, "The last thing I remember was in the hospital and thinking I could not leave Bill.

"Then the most overwhelming feeling of love, which was indescribable washed over me...I, I, uh, I was in this other place with people whom I knew and loved standing on both sides of me sending me wonderful, warm and loving thoughts, and I was moving between them being pulled by a bright light that reminded me of a tunnel! And now I am here."

Bruce smiled a tender, all-knowing smile and said, "There is much for you to learn and see and remember. Felicia and Sarah will be accompanying you on your new journey and will answer any questions you have along the way. This is a time for your recovery and awakening."

With that, each person sent her such loving thoughts that she felt as surely as if they had physically walked up and hugged her. The thoughts embraced her. Christina then turned to Felicia and Sarah and said, "Please tell me what is going on. I think I know, but if I'm right, this is not anything like what I imagined."

Felicia asked, "What is it you think?"

Christina hesitated for a moment, because she always believed that if you verbalize something it could make it happen if it was not already true.

"I believe I must have died." She then realized how foolish this must sound because here she was alive and well. In fact, this was the best she had felt in months. "But that can't be, can it?"

Sarah smiled and said, "Well, you did leave the Earth plane. However, as you can see, no one ever really dies. You are simply in another dimension where the vibrations are much higher. The dimension you are in actually overlaps the physical plane. Eventually we will show you how that works. You can see the Earth life due to the slower vibration level, but the majority of people on Earth cannot see us because of the higher vibrations we are emanating."

"If we are overlapping, how come I can't see them now?" asked Christina.

"It's very much the same as tuning in a radio. We need to fine tune the frequencies, otherwise it would be rather busy and confusing, like listening to several radio stations at the same time," commented Felicia. "In time you will learn how to do this on your own."

"But I want to do it now and see Bill and the girls and how they are doing! I've got to know. NOW!" Christina felt a sense of urgency and at the same time a feeling of despair...a longing. Much to her surprise, the feeling disappeared almost as quickly as it appeared.

"In time, you will be able to do this with ease. Right now there is much for us to show and teach you. You have much to do and we are here to help prepare you for it," stressed Sarah as she took hold of Christina's hand. There was not the least hint of impatience coming from Sarah, which surprised Christina, because in thinking back she felt she had been rather demanding and maybe even a little rude.

Sarah only smiled and said, "We understand. It is important for you to know they are exactly where they should be."

"What a strange thing to say," thought Christina. "Where they should be?"

Once again, as if reading Christina's mind Felicia answered "We all have certain paths we have chosen to follow to accomplish lifetime goals which we actually lay out for ourselves before entering the Earth plane. Although these paths can change at any time due to our free will, your husband and daughters are on the paths they have chosen. They each needed to experience the loss of a loved one. This, of course, will both tax the emotions of each in different ways, developing a new aspect of their emotional makeup; and, will instill in each a new-found strength which was previously unknown to them. This is oversimplifying the explanation in answer to your question, but in time, all these things will become clear to you as you begin to see the whole picture."

Christina, feeling confused again, asked, "Am I where I should be?"

"Of course you are!" said Sarah. "You fulfilled your life's purpose. You accomplished what you planned for yourself this lifetime. Let's look back together and see all your wonderful achievements."

CHAPTER 3

Christina was suddenly very nervous about the idea, unable to remember anything particularly significant. "Is this what they mean when they say your life flashes before you at the time of death?"

Laughing, Felicia said, "I guess it is. It helps us to understand our purpose, what lessons we learned and our debts, either paid back or owed.

"First, you and Bill are what are referred to as 'Soul Mates.' As it all starts coming back to you, you will remember many lifetimes with him before. Yes, you have been in the physical body many, many times before. Also with your daughters. There is an expression, 'We reincarnate as clusters of grapes,' meaning we have all been together in various relationships before, and we tend to return together time after time. This is true of families and friends and even people we view as 'difficult to get along with,' or think of as 'enemies.'"

Sarah interrupted saying, "We'll go into more detail about relationships and debts to refresh your memory later, because these things you already know. As we progress you will start remembering. But first things first. Let's start by looking at your early childhood. Are you ready?"

Christina hesitantly agreed to this 'look back' with slight trepidation. Sarah and Felicia each took hold of a hand and instantly, they were watching Christina as a child, as if it were a giant a movie screen. But they were there. It felt strange to see herself apart from herself, although she felt a strong pull to the Christina she was viewing and a tremendous love for her. Little Christina was very slight and fair, with strawberry-blonde braids to her waist and a skinned knee. She saw her Mommy in the kitchen cooking dinner. She and her younger brother Stephen were setting the table together and talking. They were discussing school and the kids in their classes that were "dummies and bullies." This gave Christina an instant feeling of regret for thinking of classmates in that way. Next, she saw her Father driving up into the driveway and getting out of the car to open the garage door. Christina, Stephen and Mother were all happy to see him home. That overwhelming feeling of love returned, engulfing Christina as she longed to be there instead of just watching. She was seeing a wonderful and loving childhood.

Sarah pointed out, "You were a very happy child. You were a caring and loving and thoughtful child. Expressing love is the greatest achievement in any lifetime. You and your brother were well behaved and enjoyed time spent with each other. He was very important in your life and you in his. Many lessons were shared and you both benefited in separate ways. In some instances you were his teacher and in other ways he was your teacher. Parenting is a very important, albeit sometimes difficult job, and you and your brother made it a joyful experience for your parents. No matter how simple these experiences seem, they are all definite accomplishments in your life."

As Christina watched the experiences unfold before her eyes she remembered many more. Such as the times, although rare, when her brother required a spanking from their Father. Being a very gentle man, they were never severe punishments, rather a warning. Even so, Christina would cry with her brother, wishing it would be over with quickly.

Next, she saw herself waking in the middle of the night having had a nightmare and crying uncontrollably. She had dreamed that Stephen was riding his bicycle and had been hit by a bus. Her Mother rushed to her side and held her, stroking her hair as she listened to Christina relating the terrible dream. Christina and Stephen were still sharing a bedroom, so her Mother went over and picked Stephen up from his bed and carried him to Christina placing him in her lap to hold, showing that he was all right. Christina remembered how grateful and relieved she felt at that moment while holding her brother. The love she felt for her Mother and her understanding, at that moment, was almost tangible. These feelings came flooding back to her instantly. Suddenly she missed them all so terribly. Then it struck her they had all passed over before her and must surely be here also.

"My parents and my brother! Are they here? Where are they? Can I see them?" She started condemning herself for not having thought of them sooner. Where was her mind anyway?

Felicia said "You have been through a great deal and have been recovering. Not physically, of course, but a recovery nonetheless. There remains a connection to the body after separation and it takes several days, in Earth time, for the separation to be complete. This is due to the emotional connection to our physical bodies. It is only natural for you to be in a haze for awhile. That is why we are here to help you through this period. As this memory has come back to you others will also. Yes, they are all here and are equally as anxious to see you as you are them. They have been following your progress and will reunite with you shortly.

CHAPTER 4

"You have worked hard enough since your awakening, so let's have some fun. I think you have earned it. We'll take a look around and show you some of the areas that will be of particular interest to you. First you should dress properly," Felicia said with a hint of impishness. "What was your favorite outfit to relax in or go shopping?"

Immediately a picture flashed before her mind's eye of her beige slacks and an oversized soft, green sweater that made her feel secure and comfortable. Of course, she had to have her soft walking shoes with green socks to match her sweater. She knew she was probably exceedingly fanatic about things matching, such as her socks to her tops and naturally coordinating lipstick and eyeshadow.

As soon as she conjured up this picture in her mind Sarah said, "Now concentrate on the clothing exactly as you would like it to be. While concentrating, try not to let your mind wander. Starting at your head work your way down to your toes."

After some difficulty with her active, wandering mind and having to start all over at the beginning, Christina was able to complete the task. It seemed more like a chore than the "fun" Sarah mentioned. At the giggles of both girls, Christina looked down at her feet in the direction they were pointing and saw them with green socks and walking shoes. Holding out her arms she saw they were covered with her comfortable and much-welcomed green sweater! She appeared exactly as she imagined herself during her concentration.

"How did I do that?" she asked, amazed and pleasantly surprised.

"That's how things work here. If there is something you want, you only have to create it with your mind. Imagine it, if you will," said Felicia. "Say for instance, you wanted an apple - although we don't need food here - just picture an apple in your hand and it will appear there."

This was certainly an exciting prospect for Christina and her mind was beginning to run wild about all the things she could want and create.

"Hey, hey! Slow down! You will have plenty of time to experiment and, of course, we will be here to help you.

"This act of creating is exactly the same in the physical. It is one of the things we are busy trying to teach the Earth plane. Everything, and we do mean everything, we have in the physical began as a thought. We had to think of it first before it could become a reality in our lives. The more we concentrated or meditated on it, the more quickly it materialized in our lives. This is the act of 'visualization.' As you have just seen, thoughts really are things. One of our jobs is to try to impress this truth upon the people we look after who are in the physical. We are all creators."

"Now we have some other places to show you. Exciting places. Are you ready?" Sarah asked.

Christina thought, "Of course I'm ready, what else do I have to do?" Then tried to check herself for being sarcastic, but it was too late.

"I know how you feel. I felt the same way when I came here before I realized that this was home. We are not really teaching you anything; we are only helping you to remember" said Felicia grinning at Christina's embarrassment at being "read" again. "Don't feel embarrassed, this is all a perfectly natural stage of the transition."

She took Christina's hand and they started walking. They were outside in a place that Christina felt was vaguely familiar, but the beauty was beyond anything in her recent memory. The colors were so vibrant they seemed to move. There was a fragrance in the air that made Christina giggle as she mentally described it as "heavenly."

"Is that what it is?" She asked. "Heavenly?" Suddenly she was feeling concerned as to where she was. This made both Felicia and Sarah smile at each other with an understanding of Christina's sudden concern.

"Call it whatever you wish. This is the only place there is; however, there are several levels of existence here. We can move to levels 'below' us, but we cannot move to the higher-plane levels. That is earned," answered Sarah.

Christina then looked to the sky that seemed to be the very same sky she left, except for the brilliance of the blue and the iridescence of the clouds. She felt a soft breeze that carried warmth plus, she noticed for the first time, music. Voices creating beautiful music. She found she could either shut it out or open up to it. "Who is singing, where is it coming from?" She asked.

"It is the music of the angels. When they speak it sounds as music to us, and it surrounds us all the time. As you have already observed you have the ability to shut it out. There may be other music you would like to create for your own personal pleasure. The choice is always yours. But the angelic sounds are always here for us to enjoy as we wish," said Felicia.

Christina could feel the music as it moved through her. She closed her eyes and could feel herself rising in the air. "Talk about an elevating experience," she thought. This delighted both the girls who reached up and took her hands, gently bringing her back down until her feet touched solid ground. As the three girls continued walking they came upon buildings of all types and styles, but strangely the structures did not look out of place with each other. Everything seemed a perfect blend. "As it should be," thought Christina. Again the girls looked at each other and smiled.

"What are those buildings?" Christina asked.

"The Victorian style building with the ivy and the beautiful windows is a library. We use it frequently. We don't stop learning just because we are here. There are also books provided just for pleasure. Every book ever written, even those that are still in progress on the Earth plane are here. Naturally, as we told you before, there is a specific book you want you have the ability to 'create' it with your mind, rather than coming to the library. Speaking of learning, the white marble building right next to it is full of classrooms with classes going on all the time. Choose your subject and it's available. When you are ready, the majority of classes are for the development of teachers to work with the Earth plane or do what we are doing with you right now. There are also planes other than the Earth plane to work with. Contrary to popular belief the Earth is not the only planet with life. They all need our help. And help is what we want to do," explained Sarah. "It's what we are here for. It is our chosen work for the period before we return to Earth."

That all seemed perfectly natural to Christina and she realized she 'knew' she would return to Earth sometime. This all fit in with her belief system while in her life with Bill. They had discussed the concept and studied numerous books and took classes on the subject. It simply had not occurred to Christina that it could be any other way than through the evolution of the soul. She had passed this on to her girls as a possibility and as definite 'food for thought' to be considered and studied on their own. The same way her Mother had passed it on to her. She remembered her Mother laughing and saying, "I did my level best to brainwash you about the theory of evolution." Of course she was only joking, because Christina went to churches of her own choosing and did her own investigations and independent study, in her special I-need-to-know way. She ultimately turned to the theory that made the most sense to her and the one that just felt right inside. Her parents had told her to turn within for the truth, for it was always there waiting for us to discover it. "Intuition," they had said. As with the majority of issues in

Christina's life, she realized again that they had been right. She had been so lucky to have had them as parents.

This thought was interrupted by Felicia saying, "Luck had nothing to do with it. You chose them as parents. They were exactly what you would need during your lifetime to accomplish the goals you had set for yourself and would provide you with the strength of character and purpose. There are no accidents. Your 'luck' was very carefully chosen and decided by you. In turn, they also chose you as their beloved daughter and Stephen as their son."

Christina understood this to be true. "Intuition," she could hear her Father saying. It was as though he was standing right next to her. Coming out of her reverie she turned to her right and standing there was the first, most important man in her life. The man who set the standards for all the men who tried to become a part of her life, and who failed, except for Bill. He looked at her with the most beautiful, loving smile and held out his hands to her, wanting to embrace her. She veritably flew into his arms laughing and crying at the same time. He held her, caressing her hair and kissing her forehead and she felt she had come home to her warm and caring family. She was a child again, feeling protected and loved. The wonderful childhood memories came flooding back and she didn't want to let them go.

There had always been a certain elegance about him that commanded respect from others. But well-hidden from the general populace was delightful humor which he allowed to come to the forefront among family and friends. Christina and her brother had a deep, abiding love for him along with a healthy respect.

She remembered him coming home from work in his old Studebaker and stopping at the beginning of the driveway waiting for her and her brother to come running out of the house to greet him. He would then allow them to stand on the runningboard while he slowly drove the length of the driveway to the garage. They would all enter the house from the kitchen door off the screened-in back porch. He would walk over to Mother standing at the stove and kiss her hello. Then he would kiss his children hello.

She remembered him carrying her on his shoulders to see the fireworks better. She remembered when she was young and still in grade school, he would massage her painful legs from what the doctors called rheumatism. The pains started one birthday night while at the restaurant of her choice and he sat with her legs on his lap rubbing the pain away. He was such a handsome, gentle person, and she remembered thinking as a child that he must be the smartest person in the world. As she grew older she realized he had a delightful sense of humor and was the monarch of the puns. After she married Bill, her Father lived with them when her Mother died, and he and Bill would constantly try to outdo each other with those awful puns.

The memories continued to wash over her. He would help with homework, especially the math. They would all go to the park together on picnics. One picnic, put on by his company, he and Christina joined in the three-legged race and they won! Christina took home the prize of a Raggedy Andy doll that she treasured for years. When the family went to Coney Island each year, he would take Christina, the daredevil child, on the roller coaster rides; then on the airplanes that had a rudder you could semi-steer yourself. Next would be the Ferris Wheel, and her Father would start rocking the seat when it stopped at the top and she would be so scared until he put his arm around her. Then she knew it was all okay because he would never let anything happen to her. She had always been so proud of him.

It had been so hard when he left her. Thank heaven Bill had been there to lend his strength to her when it was so desperately needed. It was hard on Bill too, because her Father was the Father that Bill had never had and he loved him dearly. Their relationship had blossomed over the five years they had lived together. He and Christina had shed tears on each other's shoulders and had found the strength there each had been seeking.

All these thoughts had passed through her mind in an instant and she found herself leaning away from her Father and staring into his eyes. How many times had she wished she could see him just one more time? Here she was seeing him alive and well and youthful-looking with his dark hair and dancing dark eyes with the wrinkles at the corners from smiling so much. Apart from looking younger, he had not changed one iota.

"I have been watching over you and Stephen and have come to you in dreams to deliver messages. I wanted you to know I was still alive and certainly extremely well. I have been attending classes and am teaching now. Your Mother always said I was a good teacher, so I guess she knew," he said to her.

"Mother! Where is she?"

"She is right here."

At that instant her Mother appeared at his side, a vision of such beauty that Christina thought for a moment she must have forgotten how beautiful her Mother was. Then she saw it was her young appearance without the ravages of cancer that she had held in her memories. The disease had created a change so slow and so subtle it was hardly noticeable. Now she saw the beauty she had known as a young child whenever she looked at her Mother. She smiled the old familiar brilliant smile that had always captivated Christina.

Christina was instantly in her Mother's arms and it felt as though she had never left them. This is a miracle, she thought. She even smelled the familiar fragrance of her Mother, subtle and comforting. Was it every Mother's smell, or just her Mother's; or do Mothers only smell that way to their children? The beautiful and artistic hands that had always amazed Christina. She would watch them work at the easel creating a wondrous likeness of people she only knew from photographs. Her Mother had always said she could not paint her own children because she knew them too well and only saw them through a loving Mother's eyes. Although she tried and tried, she did not know if she captured the way they truly appeared, or if painted them the way she saw them. The closest she came was doing silhouettes of them without features at all. Even at that there was no mistaking who they were.

Christina always thought her Mother was out of her time, being far ahead of everyone else. Her Mother was an amateur astrologer, philosopher, artist of great depth and the Mother of all Mothers, believing it to be her most important reason for being.

Again the memories came sifting through Christina's mind. Her Mother, the seamstress, making so many of her daughter's clothes...sitting up late at night making the dance recital costumes for Christina's tap and ballet classes. Her Mother made her high school prom dresses which were so much more beautiful than the uncomfortable net formals the other girls were wearing. She exercised supreme patience trying to teach Christina, though unsuccessfully, how to sew. By example she taught Christina how to be a wonderful, attentive mother herself. Although not a particularly great cook, she did teach Christina the basics in the kitchen, such as: how to measure, level off measuring spoons, separate eggs, sift flour (which Christina thought was because her Mother didn't want to do it) and, tap the bottom of the cake pan to remove all the air bubbles. Her Mother was definitely her best friend, whom she could talk to about anything. She encouraged Christina and worked hard to build up her self-confidence and esteem, which, defying all logical explanation seemed to be lacking.

They went shopping together and sometimes even went to the movies when Mother had a little extra in the money till. And they laughed together. When chaperones were needed for grade school outings, her Mother always volunteered. On two separate occasions, when Christina was in high school, her sorority would spend a weekend on a lake in the northern part of the state and both times her Mother was one of the chaperones. Each of the 15 sorority sisters came to love Christina's Mother and some even feeling close enough to call her "Mom." Some of Christina's friends were jealous of her relationship with her Mother, not having a close relationship with their own, and this puzzled Christina.

At Christmas time, Mother would make a shadow box of wonderful Christmas scenes and take such care with the decorations and especially the tree, to the point of perfectionism. Christina always thought their house was the prettiest this time of the year.

Christina would come home from school dropping her school books on the ironing board in the dining room, which always seemed to be there, anxious to tell her Mother of all the happenings of the day: the cute guy in her otherwise-useless biology class; being selected for the girls' basketball team. Christina always knew being tall would come in handy for something someday, although she had been certain it would be something much more glamorous than basketball. She remembered her Mother agonizing with her over broken relationships with the current 'most wonderful boy in the world.' But Mother always understood her pain. Mother always seemed to understand everything.

Here she was, once again the little girl in her Mother's eyes and glad to be there. The love she felt was almost tangible. The separation had seemed interminable, however, in reality it never was. Christina knew now she had always felt her Mother's presence and influence, and on many occasions it seemed she gently pushed or prodded her in the correct direction. Now she remembered her Mother coming to her in dreams that were not dreams at all, but visitations with her delivering advice or comfort. The bond is never severed and the love reaches across all barriers of the mind.

She looked at her Mother and Father standing there together and knew they had been together for a long, long time. They seemed to belong together. Obvious 'soul mates.' They both smiled at Christina and sent her love mentally and as they embraced her, no words were necessary. Everything that needed to be said was said in their embrace. It was a love eternal, never-ending.

"We must return to our teaching for now and will be back again to be with you. We will see you in class when you are ready. Your brother is there and is anxious to see you, as we know you are to see him," her Mother said, They turned and hand-in-hand walked down the path away from Christina, instead of just disappearing as people seemed to do around here.

CHAPTER 5

Instantly, Christina realized this was home and she had been away on a visit in the physical, not the other way around. She never wanted to leave again. She had been away far too long. She felt love in the air around her, and could see it in the trees and the countryside and particularly in all the people with her. The love radiated in colors that actually vibrated with soft sounds. It was all coming back to her slowly. She walked over to a nearby tree and touched the bark. It responded with a sound that was more a vibration moving through her entire body, rather than a sound you would hear when striking a piano key. This sound you felt more than heard. Each color responded with a different resonance. The deeper the color the deeper the tone; the lighter the color or shade, the higher the tone. There were colors here that had no corresponding color in the physical; they were too fine. Everything was so alive. Funny, how people are taught all their lives that this is where you would come when you "died." If you were lucky, that is! Now it seemed to Christina that you "died" when you entered the physical and had to leave this beautiful place.

Sarah once again answered her thoughts by saying, "This is our home and we visit the other planes for the experiences necessary to our development and overall growth. We as individuals are responsible for it all. We choose the life experiences, our mother and father, the greater family, our mate and our children. They all come together to provide the 'map' of our existence in the physical. We even choose when to be born so that the proper planetary alignments at the moment of our 'birth' will be an impelling influence. We can insinuate our name, or possible name combinations, into the thought processes of our parents so there will be the benefits of the best numerological influences as well. As you can see, there are no accidents. That is not to say it is fatalistic in nature, at least from the physical standpoint, because there are many different paths open to us hundreds of thousands of times during each lifetime. The right of choice is ours on the physical plane. We did, however, make the initial overall decision before making our physical appearance...."

Sarah's voice started to fade into the background of Christina's hearing. She could feel herself inexplicably being pulled in another direction. To where, she did not know. It was as though a giant magnet was aimed at her. She suddenly realized it was pulling her toward Bill and her daughters. She could still hear Sarah, but she was unable to maintain a focus on what she was saying and her words became fainter and fainter. She felt great emotional pain and the urgent need to be with her family, to comfort them. Then she was falling, falling. In the distance she heard Sarah calling to her, but somehow it did not seem important just now. She continued falling through sounds, colors, emotions, and it seemed, through time. She was experiencing a great confusion, of being displaced.

"What is happening to me?" Christina was suddenly afraid.

When the sensation of falling stopped, she was standing in the living room of her and Bill's home. He was sitting in the wing-backed chair in front of the fireplace weeping. She felt his despair and loneliness surround her. It was pulling her to him. She went over and tried to comfort him, telling him she was okay. She wanted him to know she felt wonderfully free from the months of pain. When she tried to touch his cheek her hand moved through it without making contact. However, she noticed he did stir a little and touched his cheek with his hand. Her Bill...so very handsome with his graying black hair and his tall, large frame that gave the appearance of overweight. This was deceiving, however, because he was in excellent physical shape.

She wanted so desperately to comfort him - to take away the pain. She wanted him to know about the beauty that awaited them both, one day. She wanted him to know they would be together again. But he was deaf to her voice.

"How can I get through to him?" She wondered.

At that moment the phone rang which made Bill jump and come out of his mourning mist.

"Hello."

"Hi Dad." It was Anne.

"Karen and I were wondering if we could come over for a while. We are both feeling a little lost and we were hoping it would help to be together. Would it be okay?"

"Sure, dear. I was really down tonight also. I don't think I'll be very good company, but you are both welcome to come over. I can't get your Mother out of my mind."

"We'll be right over."

After hanging up, Bill went out to the kitchen and put on a pot of coffee for the girls. It was a cold, fall evening and they will need some warming up. Christina loved this room and spent most of her spare time in here. She had decorated it with bright yellows, white cabinets and green cushions on the chairs. He thought of Christina again and how this was their favorite time of the year.

Coffee made and beginning to perk, he went back into the living room to his wing-backed chair and fell back into it, exhausted.

"Why, Christina? Why did this have to happen, just when we had everything going for us?" He felt the tears stinging his eyes. The pain was the closest thing to being unbearable that he had ever experienced.

"If only he could hear me or see me, I could show him I'm not really gone," Christina thought. There must be a way. She stood in front of Bill and willed him to see her. He did not. She shouted to him to hear her. He did not. He was too wrapped up in his misery and pain. She bent over and touched his cheek again, and again he brushed it with his hand.

At that moment the doorbell rang. It was the girls. Bill got up slowly. Christina saw he was moving so slowly that he was beginning to look like an old man. He was shuffling as though the very life was draining out of him. She had to get through to him somehow. To let him know there was not an ending, only a continuation.

He opened the heavy front door and both girls hugged him and headed for the living room and warm fireplace. They dumped their coats on the end of the couch, not bothering to hang them up and flopped down on the opposite end. Both looked very tired and had swollen eyes, red from crying. Christina reached out to them wanting to hold them both. She was their Mother, after all. They needed her! They needed her now! But no matter how hard she tried she was as invisible to them as she was to Bill.

"How frustrating and angry this makes me feel," she thought. "I need to be there for them and I can do nothing. How can I make this easier for them? I must let them know that I am not dead! I can't leave them now when they need me. I will figure out a way to get through to them."

Christina sat on the couch where the coats were and looked at her beautiful daughters.

"How are you doing Daddy?" asked Karen.

"Not well at all, I guess. I keep wondering where I go from here. What do I do with the rest of my life. Your Mother and I were so much a part of each other that half of me is gone and I seem to have lost my drive. I don't feel a need to accomplish anything. I guess I always needed a reason to excel and your Mother was that reason."

"Mother would want you to go on, you know," said Anne. "But I know the feeling of missing part of yourself. I pick up the phone during the day and start dialing her number before I realize she's not there to answer. Then I sit there and cry. I am certainly not as productive as I was before."

"I know," said Karen. "I do the same thing. The other day I was driving past the art museum and remembered the times going there with Mom and thought I would call her to see if she wanted to go with me this weekend. When it occurred to me what I was doing, I broke down and cried so hard I had to pull off on the side of the road until I calmed myself down. How are we going to get a grip on these emotions? How long is it going to take to get past this?"

"I don't know," said Bill. "How about some coffee? I made some for you since it's so cold outside."

"I'll get it." Anne got up and went out to the kitchen and grabbed three mugs from the cupboard. She reached for the small decorated tray standing up on the counter that she had given her Mother one Mother's Day many years ago. She felt a sharp pain in her chest that seemed to be directly connected to her tear ducts, which began flowing. Trying to gain control she wiped her eyes on her sleeve and poured coffee into each cup and carried the tray out to the living room. As she offered her Dad his cup he noticed she had been crying again. He smiled a weak, but understanding smile and nodded slightly to her.

Christina reached out to Anne and touched her arm, patting it. Anne was unaware of her mother's effort to comfort her.

"If only I could reach them some way. How can it be done? I have read many stories of encounters with 'ghosts,' and unsolicited help from the 'other side.' Why am I incapable of reaching the people I love the most? It doesn't make sense. If I am not here to help, then why am I here? It seemed as though I was called here for some reason. The pull I experienced was a very real thing. I must be here to help them, so how am I supposed to accomplish that? I can't even make my presence known to them. It must take more than a strong desire. What am I to do? Who is there to help me? I must help them," Christina pleaded.

No answer was forthcoming.

"Have I been abandoned? Where are all the people that were there to help me?" Christina asked herself, feeling not only alone, but afraid for the first time. "If I am unable to do anything here, how do I get back to Sarah and Felicia?"

There was no one there to read her thoughts this time; therefore, there were no answers to her questions or her fears.

Bill, sitting in his chair staring into nothingness, was running his fingers along the side of his head, and then down the back of his neck and letting his hand rest there, as he did when he was lost in thought. He was a professor at the college nearby and loved by his students because of his sense of humor and the ability to make any intellectual journey as exciting as an African Safari. He would to tell them, "Whatever your ultimate goal, it's the journey getting there that is the greatest teacher and the most fulfilling." He tried to make that journey fascinating for each student.

His classrooms were never classes made up of kids, but they were individuals with names making up the classes. He prided himself on knowing each one of their names and with many, something personal about them. He regarded them all with respect and was given respect in return by all. His colleagues often heard him say he always left his classroom with a little more than he went in with. He believed he learned a lot from his students. His sense of humor kept him in the league of favorites.

"Since your mother has gone, I have difficulty even getting up in the mornings. I fight myself to get ready for school. Once there, I have trouble concentrating on the class material. My students are suffering and it's my fault. Maybe I need to take a sabbatical. I'm not fulfilling my obligation to them and certainly not keeping it interesting or challenging. My biggest challenge is just getting through the day," Bill told his daughters.

As though it was a movie, Christina could see how much more Bill had to give his students and the wonderful contributions he had yet to make. She must let him know somehow. "He absolutely cannot give up like this. It isn't natural for him to lose his incentive and shortchange his students. And those girls! They need to let go of this grief and get on with their lives with their husbands. And the beautiful children I see in their futures. Good grief! Somehow I have to stop this mourning. It's unhealthy to continue it and it is destructive. I guess that's 'bad grief!' To think I did the same thing when I lost my parents. Did they agonize over me the same way as I am now? I am sure they must have. I'll have to remember to ask them when I get back...if I get back." Christina was now floating above her family in the living room and moving back and forth between the girls and Bill. She could feel herself becoming increasingly agitated, and frustrated at not being able to 'get through' to them.

Christina had to have faith in Bill and his keen abilities. "I am convinced that eventually he will come around and re-familiarize himself with his smartness. I could not have been that wrong about him. I was also too smart for that."

She swished past them trying to stir up a breeze that would get their attention. Instead Bill got up and added another log to the fire saying something about it dying down. She tried swishing again, but this time Anne stood up and putting on her coat said it was time to return home to her patient husband. Karen agreed it was time to leave and hugged and kissed her Father good-bye and wished him a restful sleep.

CHAPTER 6

After they left, Bill carried the coffee cups to the kitchen. Before he turned out the lights, he stood there visualizing Christina standing at the kitchen sink smiling. He remembered the many wonderful times they had in that kitchen over cups of coffee. They shared each day's events sitting at the kitchen table. He recalled the meals with the girls and listening to their love problems, the latest exams, and the new teacher that was so 'dumb,' by their teenage standards, of course. In his mind's eye, he could see the four of them laughing and loving and sharing. It seemed like several lifetimes ago. He could hear all the voices echoing in his mind. He returned to the living room to spread out the logs a little in the fireplace, before retiring.

Christina followed him upstairs to their bedroom. Bill prepared for bed then climbed in and stared at the ceiling without turning out the light. Christina could see his thoughts, which were memories of their times together. Curled up on the couch together in front of the fire. Karen and Anne playing on their swing set in the back yard when they were 5 and 6 years old and Christina taking turns pushing each one. Bill flipping hamburgers on their backyard grill. "It was good," she thought.

Bill finally rolled over and turned out the light, pulling the covers up around his neck. Christina lay down on the bed next to him as much for her comfort as his. She did not feel the need for sleep, just the need to be close to him again.

As he moved into a deep sleep, she saw movement. He was sitting up. At first he startled her, but then she realized he was sitting up but his body was still lying on the bed in deep sleep. He was leaving his body. He started drifting upwards and she drifted upwards with him. He turned and saw her and joy replaced grief on his face. They held hands and floated around the room together. They spoke without words. She led him through the bedroom wall as if it were not there. She took him down to their beloved river and in silence they walked the shore. The cold did not affect them since there were no bodies involved.

"Bill, you must go on without me. As you can now see, we are together. I am not 'dead,' but very much alive. You have much to do. I will be here for you every night during your sleep state. We are not ever really separated. I want you to remember this experience tomorrow; however, I know that is probably not what you will remember of this. Tonight will come back to you as a disjointed dream, but the essence of it will remain."

"Christina, I know all this. It's just that the physical memory acts as a filter and the finer elements slip away leaving only that which we can relate to on a physical level. I also know I must go on, that I have things to do yet; otherwise I would be where you are now. It's back in the wakeful state without this memory that makes it so difficult, when the personality takes over camouflaging the inner knowledge of the soul. Perhaps with working in meditation during the day, I can learn to remember these moments."

They spent additional time together soaring over their small town and traveling the river. Neither of them wanting this moment to come to an end. They took a turn from the river and heading north flew over Anne's house, which was silent in sleep. Just three blocks away was Karen's house, also in slumber. Knowing they were both in peaceful sleep helped Christina ease the feelings of anxiety about them.

"I guess it's just as hard for me to let go as it is for you," she said to Bill.

"I think it's an ego thing. We got used to the idea of 'belonging' to each other and now the ego does not want to let go of that idea. No matter how wrong it is. It is ego dictating our emotions, instead of our letting the Self or Soul come through," he replied. "Love is a bridge that will always bring us together. Not because we belong to each other, but a universal love of our Higher Selves."

"I just wish I could make it easier for you during the day some way, so you wouldn't have to suffer so much," Christina said.

"If you were able to make it easier for me, then the experience would not offer me the opportunity for growth. From this vantage point I can see what I must learn from this experience. My life has been without too many challenges. Things have come easily for me. I was always smart, got good grades without overtaxing myself, and fell into jobs that filled a current need. Even the college teaching job came easily. I have always done what I love to do.

"You were always there for me as my confidant, my sounding board, my best friend, my reinforcement whenever needed. Now I will be on my own to be my own best friend, and my own reinforcement. I will have to develop an emotional strength to be called upon, which has been virtually unknown to me. For the first time in my life I am going to have to strenuously work at something that will not be particularly pleasant or easy for me. True, when you were so ill and in the hospital it was a very unpleasant and difficult time for me, but it was a temporary situation in the scope of things. What I am facing now will be a long-term process which will bring with it many more opportunities
to fall on my face, but allow me to get up stronger. In short, in many areas you were my strength. I never had to do it on my own. Until now.

"So, my love, I don't want you to make it easier for me. Easy is not always best. This way I won't have to face this situation, or another like it, at another time. I am being given this opportunity to do it now and do it right! And I intend to do just that." Bill was being very emphatic about this leaving Christina with nothing to say.

They continued holding hands and soaring over the farms, the gentle foothills and the heart of town. Heading back home, Christina said, "I will be here again tomorrow night and continue to stay with you even if you are unaware of me when you are awake."

Together, they drifted into the bedroom and for the first time Christina noticed the silver cord connecting Bill to his sleeping body. She had heard of the silver cord but did not recall ever having seen it. The cord connected the physical body to the astral body and only severed at the time of death. It was at this thought she realized she indeed did not have a cord. She did not have a body to connect it to. The whole idea made her laugh at herself. "I don't have a cord, because I don't have a body," she said to Bill pointing at his life support system shining and silver. "I don't have anything to go back to - I am what I am. Think about it. I am completely free with no encumbrances. The thought of going back to that restrictive, heavy body and feeling the pull of gravity is not one I cherish. To say nothing of the freedom from sickness and pain. It's really great! I don't think I ever want to go back. Maybe I can continue to grow and learn on the other side."

"Maybe you can," said Bill. "I have heard that people who have had near-death experiences say the same thing. They don't want to come back to the physical. That the freedom they feel is not something they want to give up."

They both landed back in bed where they continued to talk until the morning light.

CHAPTER 7

Bill awoke with the alarm and instead of willing the day to be over, he strangely felt as though he did not mind getting up.

"This is odd," he thought. "I almost feel good today. After last night with Anne and Karen I thought I would be exhausted and not feel like going to work as usual."

He shuffled into the bathroom to shave, feeling as though something important had happened. Although he could not put his finger on it.

"Maybe with time it does become more tolerable," he said to himself in the mirror. However, he thought he sure didn't look that great. His eyes were puffy from tears and face looked swollen to match.

"Well, this should sure cheer the kids up this morning! They love to have a reason to laugh at you behind your back. Hunt no further, the brunt of your jokes is here," he said to himself, laughing for the first time in months. The sound of his own laughter startled him as though it were a stranger.

"I guess it has been a long time. Six months with no laughter is a long time. Especially from someone who always found a reason to laugh every day. No wonder I look so awful!" he admonished himself.

He showered and dressed and made his way to the kitchen for his toast and cup of coffee. While waiting for his toast he turned around half expecting to see Christina pouring his coffee. It was the same feeling as when she was alive of not having to see her to feel her presence when she entered the room. They were in tune with each other and alert to each other's vibrations.

"Good morning, sweetheart," he said just in case his first impression was right.

Christina smiled at him from over his coffee cup. "Good morning, dear," she responded.

Bill left for work with anticipation for the first time in six months. This was a good day.

CHAPTER 8

Christina drifted over the Anne's house and watched her dress for work. She tried hard to impress her with her presence, but to no avail. Anne was depressed, but not so overwhelmed with it as her father. "She's a pretty strong little girl," thought Christina. "She seems able to get a handle on it and not let it rule her day. You have so much potential and so much to offer the world, Anne. You will be successful in all that you do," Christina told her deaf ears. Deaf or not, Anne smiled.

Anne had always been willful and had to do things for herself instead of listening to parental advice. Christina had found it rather difficult to watch her make her mistakes and not say anything. She had felt that since she had already made the mistakes, it would enable her to prevent Anne or Karen from duplicating them. If it didn't work that way... it should! And obviously it didn't. At least in Anne's case. Anne didn't go to college, because she just wanted to get married and have children. Why on earth should she need college for that?

No matter how hard Christina tried to reason with Anne, telling her that one day she may need her education to fall back on, it was to no avail. Anne always "knew better." Now she was married and instead of motherhood, she was working as a hostess at a local restaurant. One of the better restaurants mind you, but a restaurant nonetheless. They are saving for a home in which to start their family and John could not do it on his single salary. One of the little things about which Anne had not given much thought.

Anne was tall and slender and extremely pretty with an open nature that broadcasted friendliness to everyone she met. This would certainly stand her in good stead in the restaurant business. It also attracted her wonderful husband John, whom Christina was so very fond of. His whole life seemed to be centered around Anne and whatever she wanted was okay with him. Christina always thought his generosity was the means to Anne becoming more spoiled than she already was. From her new vantagepoint, however, Christina saw that Anne would indeed become the mother she had dreamed of being and her current circumstances were only temporary.

Next, it was time to check in on Karen. Although the younger child, she always had an inner strength that saw her through all her difficult times. It seemed she was born knowing who she was without having to be told. No one had to teach her self-esteem. She just accepted it and approached life in a pragmatic fashion. Christina always felt this coupled with her outrageous sense of humor would see her through anything. Anything at all. It did seem as though she was handling her mother's departure better than anyone else was. Life would always be good to her because of her wonderful attitude. She was unflappable and saw the humor in just about everything. "A very wise and loving soul," Christina thought.

Karen 'lucked' into a really good job in an office setting that paid well, enabling her to go to college at night working toward her degree in interior design. She had a natural creative sense, which showed in her and Scott's apartment. Small things such as the placement of pictures on the wall or the unusual use of color or flower arrangements in a way that Christina never would have thought of. "It is a special talent - a gift," Christina thought in admiration.

Christina loved both her daughters so very much and she delighted in the way they grew up and became such incredible young women. Any mother would be proud.

"I love you Mom, and I dedicate this day to you," Karen said as she walked out the door.

CHAPTER 9

"You know, I don't think I did a bad job at all with my family," Christina told herself. "I am glad to know they are independent enough to get along without me, which was one of my aims raising them.

"Think I'll go visit some of my old haunts," she said laughing at her terrible joke.

She could have just thought about the place she wanted to be and the thought itself would transport her there. Instead, however, she preferred the floating feeling and the trip that was so much like flying. She could view all the things going on below her along the way and was a welcomed diversion. She could see old friends walking on the sidewalk below heading for their favorite coffee shop for lunch. She 'dropped' in to see them and a wave of nostalgia came over her wishing she could sit with them and enjoy the banter they all shared. They looked wonderful to her and she noticed for the first time they were all radiating a light of colors around themselves.

"Auras," she said excitedly. "They are beautiful. I had no idea they looked like that."

Each one was different and she realized she could tell the mood and feelings being expressed as she watched the colors change during their animated conversation. She watched her friends and when they would become more excited, the colors would change more rapidly. The major color in all of them was blue and Christina remembered from things she had read that blue was for communication, and they were certainly communicating. Now that she was aware of the auras, she went outside the coffee shop and looked around at everyone on the streets and the sight was remarkable. You could almost read their thoughts by looking at the color changes.

She saw a woman standing at the ready teller at the bank with a dull green aura mixed with washed out yellows and Christina interpreted that the woman had money problems and was feeling guilty about withdrawing more cash from her already-low account.

A gentleman had bright oranges and blues that were ever changing and very active telling Christina that he was very creative and probably a writer or a songwriter, but definitely had his current project foremost on his mind at the moment.

She went to the local park that had a small pond with ducks and cormorants and saw that even they had auras. In fact, when turning full circle where she stood, she saw the light emanating from the trees, the evergreens and shrubs.

"It's the Divine spark of life that is in all things. It is what we are truly made of! Without it, we would not exist. The light starts at the center of our being and radiates outward and our physical bodies cannot contain it all. What I am seeing is the overflow of the life energy or spirit of each person and thing," she thought excitedly, reveling in her discovery.

"I always knew this to be true logically, but until now I just didn't grasp the full power of this truth, and how by sharing this same light we are all one," she marveled. The joy of the moment carried her up into the air and she floated above it all as a Fall leaf falling from a tree arcing from side to side and drifting silently down to Earth again. The joy she felt in her heart was almost painful and she wanted to sing, to dance.

"I can't wait to get home and tell Bill about this! He must know about this so that he can tell the girls." The thought transported Christina to their living room and the memory of last night with the frustration of not being able to be heard by her family, was delivered like a blow.

"I have to tell them about this and let them know it all okay. That we are never apart, that we are all one. It is too important, I must find a way," she shouted urgently into the empty room.

She sat on the couch and buried her head in her hands. She felt a presence in the room trying to comfort her and when she looked up she saw Tippy, their little Terrier, and he was looking directly at her wagging his tail. "He can see me!" She exclaimed. He jumped up trying to lick her and wound up licking the couch cushions and whimpered with a look of surprise. Christina talked to him mentally and Tippy responded by calming down immediately.

Christina had heard that animals could see and hear things beyond human senses. She reached over and petted him, stroking his wiry hair and he looked at her with eyes filled with unconditional love and he always had when she was "alive." The act of petting him was more a mental exercise than actual "hands on," but he was responding to her attentions nonetheless.

"The power of the mind," she thought to herself. "I have always been taught that thoughts were things. That we created with our thoughts and because of that we should keep our thoughts in check. I was always told each thought went into the ethers as an image to remain there forever and the more we held that thought the more we gave it substance. Give it enough attention and we bring it into the physical plane as real and solid as an oak table." At this remembrance Tippy was cocking his head sideways with that funny little quirky smile out of one side of his mouth, as though he completely understood. He wagged his tail and tried to nudge her knee, instead making contact with the cushion again. She reassured him by mentally patting him on his head, which seemed to satisfy his injured composure.

"Everything that exists on the Earth plane began as an idea or thought first. We had to create it with our minds first for it to exist. What an exciting revelation," she said to her avid listener. "I had even heard of two or even three people coming up with the same invention at the same time. This was probably due to the fact that someone put the idea out into the Universe and others, being very receptive, picked up the idea out of the ethers, at the same time, and acted on it. Hence several people with the 'same' idea.

"Even with something so simple as our homes. When we first see our new home we visualize how we want our living room to look, right down to the paint on the walls, the flower arrangements, the pictures on the wall and the placement of the furniture. We have just 'created' our living room. We then move on to each room of the house doing the same procedure over and over. We may have done the same thing in the building of the house. We had to create the house in our mind first and then relayed that image to the architect, who then created it in his mind before putting in on paper. Through the combined creative efforts of all the parties, the house becomes your home.

"The point is, Tippy, this creating works on intangibles as well. We create love and send it out to an individual and they will receive that positive energy from you. However, ill will sent to someone is received as well, but as negative energy. Whatever we send out comes back to us tenfold. So we should be more like you Tippy, and only send out love. It is obviously the natural way. You don't have ill will for anyone, do you? Why should we? We are all put on Earth to accomplish the same thing. We are all working toward the same goals. By helping someone else, we in turn help ourselves."

Tippy whined in agreement and turned around three times to curl up on the floor at Christina's feet, which he could see, but not feel.

Christina sat engulfed in her thoughts and found herself wishing to be back with Sarah and Felicia. She knew that was home and this merely a stopping off place. But how to get back was the big question. What was holding her here? At that moment she heard the key in the lock and Bill came in the front door. She could tell instantly from his appearance, he was feeling down again. His head was hanging down and his shoulders were stooped and he shuffled when he walked. His emotions hit her with full force. They were quite real to her and felt as though someone had hit her in the chest with a heavy pillow. It felt heavy...burdensome. He was doing this to her.

"I know he wouldn't do this, if he knew how it affected me. This is the worst I have felt since I left here. How can I make him stop?" Christina tried sending him thoughts of comfort, but he was too wrapped up in his own negative feelings to receive anything from her. It was as though his despondency has built a concrete wall around him as protection. It protected him all right, but it also shielded him from any outside help. Christina also noticed his aura was not at all beautiful as she knew it would be under normal circumstances. The colors were there, but they were washed out and in some cases darkened instead of brilliant color.

"He has got to stop doing this to himself!" Christina felt such love and compassion for him, but it was mixed with feelings of exasperation. "And to me. He's doing it to me also, without realizing it." She wanted to run from it, but was unable to do so. As much as she loved Bill and wanted to help him, she felt trapped by him. It was not at all a pleasant experience. She watched him flop down in his chair without even taking off his coat. He stared off into space with no expression on his face.

Tippy came over to him to have his ears scratched and Bill didn't even see him. Tippy looked at Christina with a knowing, sad expression. Bill had been sitting in his chair for 45 minutes when the phone rang. He didn't jump up to answer it, but let it ring about six times before slowly getting out of his chair and heading toward the kitchen wall phone. It was Karen.

"How are you Dad? I had you on my mind and decided to call and check on you."

"Okay, sweetie. It's funny, I got up feeling really good this morning for the first time in months. I was eager to get to class, but as the day wore on I started losing it. I got more depressed by the hour and couldn't get your Mother out of my mind. I felt as though we had been together again and she left me. Don't worry about me. I'm just really tired and think I'll just grab a sandwich and go to bed early. I'll talk to you tomorrow.

Thanks for calling and checking up on me. I love you." Bill hung up and stood there for a moment analyzing his feelings and his day.

This is not easy," he said to the air around him. "Since I woke up feeling good this morning, Christina and I must have spent some time together last night. I don't remember dreaming about her, but I have the overwhelming sense that something happened that was different."

With that he opened the refrigerator door looking for some dinner and found one hot-dog that looked as though it had been hiding in that drawer a few days too long. He pitched it in the disposer and continued looking. No leftovers left over. He grabbed for the block of cheese and decided on a grilled cheese sandwich.

"Not the greatest," he thought, "but it will have to do."

While it was browning in the skillet he made himself a cup of hot chocolate. He wanted something warm and was afraid the much-preferred coffee would keep him awake. And in the event he had spent last night with Christina, he didn't want to take any chances on not being able to sleep, in case he would spend time with her again tonight. He carried his too-brown-on-one-side grilled cheese sandwich and his hot chocolate into the living room and spoke to Tippy.

"I know you miss her too, boy. But somehow we will get through this." Tippy wagged his tail and started to nudge Bill's knee, but stopped and backed off and studied him, as though wondering if his nose would make contact with Bill's chair instead. Deciding to chance it, he nudged Bill and was rewarded with a hearty scratch behind his ears. Bill shared his over-done sandwich with Tippy, who did not mind the darkened bread at all. After all, it was people-food and that was better than anything else.

Bill cleaned up after himself in the kitchen, put some food down for Tippy and made his way upstairs. He was tired and cold and decided a hot shower may help him to relax and drift off to sleep more easily. After climbing into bed, he went over the day's events in his mind trying to recall when his mood starting going downhill. Without coming to any solid conclusion, he drifted off to sleep. Christina was there waiting for him.

They embraced and took flight down to their river, holding hands. As in the physical days, they talked about their day's events. Christina anxious to tell him about the auras and her realization about creating, and Bill relating his day of classes.

"I know I allowed my emotions to take over today during a slow period at school. As long as I kept busy I did all right. Unfortunately I allowed my overactive mind to get the best of me when things slowed down after class. The thing that puzzles me is that I know you are still very much alive, and that the situation is only temporary until we are together again, but in the meantime, I find our separation unbearable. Knowledge doesn't necessarily make it easy."

Christina opened her mouth to speak, but Bill spoke for her, "I know...if it was easy, I wouldn't be learning anything. If I could just remember this moment during my waking hours tomorrow. I know that would help me. Although it's obvious I did remember something this morning when I got up in a good mood, looking forward to work. It's the awareness I am looking for."

"Bill, I will help you any way I can. If you could try to become a little more receptive instead of building that wall around you for protection. You shut me out. Maybe a few more nights like this together and your moments of awareness will become longer. But for me, it is also painful, because your depression and hanging on to me, prevents me from helping you or even myself. I carry your depression around like a big weight. I cannot reach you when you are in that state of mind. I tried. Actually I would be with you more if you were able to keep your spirits up. That was bad enough to have been one of yours or Dad's puns. Maybe that's where that expression came from," Christina said, laughing.

"Anyway, you are going to have to work on yourself to ward off the deep depressions that keep us apart," Christina scolded. Then she squeezed his arm and pulled herself closer to him in a form of a hug. "It's okay. I probably wouldn't do any better myself if the roles were reversed. In fact I imagine I would be a total basket case, unable to go to work and face the world. I know you are trying very hard. I will continue to send you messages and help during your day and try to break down that barrier you worked so hard at building. Try to ease up a bit. I am so exhausted. I have been unable to get back where I belong. I have tried, but seem to be stuck here. And believe me, if you saw it there you would want to get back as soon as possible, too. It's our real home and it seems I have been away forever. I look forward to the time we can be there together."

CHAPTER 10

Bill looked at her and smiled that warm, loving smile that still thrilled her. They drifted back to bed and Bill's spirit left her, so that even though he was beside her on the bed, she was alone. In thinking back on their conversation she recalled saying she was exhausted, a fact that until now had escaped her.

"I shouldn't feel tired. I shouldn't feel anything so physical. But for some reason I do feel heavy somehow. What on earth is causing this?" She asked herself.

"It's what's on Earth that is causing it," an unknown voice said to her.

She shot up off the bed like a bullet and turned around looking for the voice that seemed to fill the entire room. She saw no one, but she did see an extremely bright light just above her.

"Who's there? Who is that talking to me? Where did you come from?"

"It is I who is talking to you from where you are supposed to be," said the voice coming from the center of the light. "You really got yourself tangled up here, didn't you?"

"I tried to get back, but for some reason I have been unable to leave here."

"I know. I have been with you through the entire ordeal. Matter of fact, I have been with you, for the most part, since the day you were born. Well, actually even before that. I am your angel. I should say one of your angels, for you have several. I have watched you grow and develop into the beautiful young woman that you became. You have done well.

"I was with you through the chicken pox, measles and took care of you during the dangerous bout with strep throat when you were nine years old. I caught you when you fell off the swings at the playground so you only got a skinned knee instead of a broken leg.

"There was the time I warned you of a car running a stop sign on your way to work. You accepted it as a premonition that made you slow down for reasons unknown to you at the time. Which it was, of course.

"At the births of both your beautiful daughters, I was there. I stood next to you at your marriage to Bill. Also, I have been watching you struggle with your current predicament. We don't normally interfere unless specifically asked to do so. But I took your questioning as a form of asking for help."

With that the voice took the form of a beautiful, tall, black man dressed in a comfortable looking pair of slacks and white, short-sleeved shirt unbuttoned at the neck, and a pair of most earth-like loafers.

His appearance made Christina smile, thinking he was trying to make her at ease by not looking like an angel, but like a modern-day human. He smiled back at her look of amusement.

"Hi, my name is Josef and I am here to help you get back. That is, if you want to go back."

"Oh, yes! I have been trying but appear to be stuck," Christina said while unable to take her eyes off her angel. "How come you don't look like an angel, and where are your wings?" She asked trying not to sound impertinent.

"Just trying to fit in, dear one. I could have come to you in my full angel attire and made a grand entrance, but in your state at the moment felt it would have been a bit much," he said with his eyes laughing and full of good humor. "See?"

With that he instantly changed his appearance in keeping with Christina's idea of what an angel should look like. He stood before her with his dark skin surrounded in glowing white robes and feathery wings that rose above his head and touched the floor. Each and every feather was distinct and perfect and had an iridescent quality to it. He was at least seven feet tall!

"What an impressive being," she thought to herself.

"Thank you, dear one. Now back to your current problem. I have some things to show and teach you. But first, let me slip into something more comfortable."

In a blink of an eye he was back in the earthly attire he had first shown Christina.

"Do you know why you are here?" He asked her.

"No. I somehow just ended up here while Sarah was talking to me."

"You are here because of your strong emotional ties to your husband and your daughters. It is a very natural occurrence. You were pulled to them by their grieving for you. Grief is a very strong emotion and one that generally requires comforting by someone. That someone would naturally be you. Grieving is a natural process by which humans heal themselves after the loss of a loved one. However, an extraordinarily long or prolonged period of grief can bring about adverse effects. As you have already experienced. It draws the loved ones back to them preventing them from going on to their next, very important phase after Earthly departure. It is what is commonly referred to as being Earthbound, where the spirit of the deceased remains on Earth to be near their loved ones.

"Now I know this was not your intent, but their grieving, and Bill's in particular, has drawn you back to them and is holding you here. You feel you must help them, comfort them, and make them understand that you are not 'dead.' It hurts you to see them in such pain, when you feel fine. Also the fact that you can see them and they cannot see you, does not help you. Except for Tippy, of course.

"I will teach you how to check on them from time to time and go home without needing my outside help. You will be able to flit back and forth as much and as often as you like. Without getting 'stuck,' I might add. I have been watching how much you have awakened your knowingness since you have been here, and it has been good. Your innate awareness is coming back to you through this experience. Of course, you would have remembered it on the other side as well, but here you discovered it on your own. It's time for a little healing now."

Josef slowly unfolded his giant, graceful wings, which had been curled up and hidden in his back and gently wrapped them around Christina in a protective manner. Christina instantly felt at peace, protected with an overwhelming feeling of well being.

"I'm in good hands now," she told herself.

CHAPTER 11

Christina felt herself drifting upward and outward. There was an unmistakable feeling of oneness with all living things as she was covered with loving warmth like hot-fudge on a sundae. It was a feeling she never wanted to let go of or be without again. When Josef opened his winged arms she was standing with Sarah and Felicia and Sarah was still talking.

"...of the basic attributes and qualities we would have to work with," Sarah continued.

"My word! Time has stood still here! But I have been gone for several days. I know I have. I remember spending two wonderful nights with Bill down at the river and our discussions. But here, I haven't missed a thing," Christina thought to herself. "Maybe I just imagined it all."

"No, my child. It did happen just the way you remember it."

Christina spun around and sure enough, there was Josef standing behind her looking beautiful beyond words, and smiling that loving smile at her.

"What has you rather confused is the time issue. In reality there is no time. All things happen at once. Time is an Earth element and your life there was governed by the linear time you all have come to know and love. Time is used to measure your events, your days, since the Earth itself measures its existence in days. Time is necessary for your life experiences. Time only exists there, however, not here," Josef said in a calm manner.

At the sound of his melodic voice, both Sarah and Felicia greeted him in a somewhat honorific way. As they nodded to him, they reached out their hands and Christina could see the white light moving from being to being. The air was charged with pure, loving energy.

"You all know each other," Christina said with a surprised squeak in her voice.

"Yes, we have all been together and with you for a very long time. We have been guides to you both individually and together," Felicia responded. "Josef has others he looks after also, but Sarah and I are all yours and have been almost since the beginning."

With this comment she bowed her head and did a little curtsy to Christina. Falling into the lighthearted mood she curtsied back to the two girls. Each hugged her in turn.

"I was gone for a few days and Josef came and rescued me and brought me back here to you," an excited Christina told them. "I tried to get back but couldn't. I thought I was not going to see you again. I felt myself being hurled into space and found myself back in my living room with Bill. I didn't do it on purpose. I just ended up there."

"You weren't ever really gone from here, Christina. There is no time here, so what seemed as a long time to you was no more than a blink of an eye to us," Sarah answered.

"So that must be why you were finishing what you were saying when I left, when I returned! I didn't know how in the world that happened! Or should I say 'how in heaven that happened.' I was really confused and thought I had imagined it."

Josef explained, "You were pulled back to Earth by the strong emotions of a grievous nature, and were not equipped to counter them; therefore, you reacted to your love of family by allowing yourself to be drawn to them uncontrollably. This happens frequently to new arrivals that had strong family ties. It is natural to grieve, but sustained grief can be harmful to both parties. When you returned to Earth, you entered into a time warp, moving from a timeless state into their linear time state. As I said earlier, I will teach you how to return at will and look in on your family from time to time, protecting yourself from being pulled back at their will.

"It was an unfortunate incident and we should have been alerted to the signs when your mind started wandering. We should have noticed your 'signal' getting weaker, so to speak. But we will be keep a keen eye on you until you become more acclimated to your new surroundings. You see, our caring for you never ends, no matter where you are."

"Before we start on that, let's get you settled somewhere," Felicia suggested. "You can create a place for yourself to go, relax and be comfortable, and to meditate and to work. And, of course, by creating I mean to create it in your mind. Picture for yourself the place you want to spend your quiet time. Your space in which to be alone," Sarah said.
"You mean I can have whatever I want?" asked Christina.

"If it is more that you have earned the right to have, then you will find yourself working against yourself. You can only create that which you have earned. Try it and see what happens," Felicia suggested.

"How do I start? I am not sure what I want. What if I conjure up something I don't like and want to change?" Christina asked with an edge to her voice.

"First, let's find a place for a setting that you like," suggested Felicia.

The three girls headed off to the right behind the school and the library where the terrain was a little hillier. Christina found an area that was not what you would call a valley, but it was definitely nestled between two hills with her beloved mountains off in the near distance. What tugged at her the most was the stream running between the hills.
"How about this? Would this be all right? Do you think anyone would mind if I selected this place?" she asked.

"Of course it would be all right and of course no one would mind. As a matter of fact it has probably just been sitting here waiting for you to choose it," offered Felicia.

"In the same way you clothed yourself and selected what you wanted to wear, you will build your home. What do you want? How about a garden? What color do you want your house? How do you want it furnished?" instructed Sarah. "Get a clear picture in your mind after thinking about what would make you feel comfortable. Give it some thought. Then close your eyes and start creating. It's simple and it won't hurt a bit. If there is something you want changed - now or later - simply change it."

Christina closed her eyes and instantly saw a large living room with dark hardwood, with two over-stuffed sofas with extra pillows, a large stone fireplace, and a very necessary window seat, with cushions and pillows in front of a bay window with diamond-shaped panes. There were tables with plants, and plants hanging from the beamed ceiling, tiffany lamps, small area rugs and a small desk in the corner. And, of course, in front of the fireplace, the wing-backed chair Bill loved so much.

All this loveliness was in rich shades of greens and purples with white accents. Warm and cozy and definitely relaxing, she thought. No point in picturing a bedroom, since sleep is not required, or a kitchen for pretty much the same kind of reasoning. There were fresh flowers strategically placed, and beautiful scenes in dark frames hanging on the walls. Outside she envisioned a crooked sidewalk with a myriad of flowers on either side, ablaze with color. Her house was cream colored with dark blue shutters at the windows and flower boxes planted with small red geraniums. She was very pleased with her image. She opened her eyes and stood staring at the image in front of her. It beckoned her inside.

She looked to the girls for direction. They nodded and smiled their approval so she strolled up the crooked walk, taking time to smell and admire her flowers. They seemed to acknowledge to her as she passed them, and their fragrance was unlike anything she had ever known on Earth. They radiated an essence that matched their beautiful colors and filled the air around them as well as anyone who came near.

She reached for the knob on the heavy oak door with the diamond-shaped windowpanes and noticed the doorknocker was an angel, in brass. This made her smile; an added touch from someone other than herself. She turned around and saw Josef grinning at her and he motioned her inside, as a mother shooing her children away from a freshly baked batch of cookies.

As she entered the large one-room cottage, it took her breath away. It was exactly as she pictured it in her mind, but with embellishments just thrown in for extra measure. The colors were the same but more vibrant; the over-stuffed sofas were fuller, fluffier. One entire wall was a dark-stained built-in bookcase filled with her favorite books dating from the present all the way back to her childhood. Mother Goose, Winnie-the-Pooh, Nancy Drew. Books she had read to her girls as small children and, of course, the books that she had been able to 'escape in' as an adult. She realized that reading had been a very important and large part of her life. A fact that she had never really thought much about before. Obviously, that is why the bookcase was here, even if she had not visualized it intentionally. Or did she do it at all?

Unable to resist any longer, she strolled over to one of the sofas and sat down, feeling caressed by the large cushions.

As beautiful and comfortable as it was, there was still something missing. "I know! My piano!" No sooner thought, appearing in the right hand corner of her room was a small grand piano, all in natural woods and stunning. It seemed to be beckoning her. In a state of wonder, she slowly walked over to her new piano and ran her fingers over the keys. The sounds coming out were unlike any piano she had ever heard on Earth. There was clarity, a brilliance, a resonance, making the Earth music sound crude and shallow. She knew a lot of time would be spent sitting right here.

She pulled out the bench, sat down and began playing one of her favorite pieces that had always given her some difficulty, Rachmaninoff's Prelude in C Sharp Minor. Instead of any difficulty or mistakes on her part, her fingers touched the keys as though they were butterflies. Without any hesitation, stress or tiring, she breezed through even the most technical areas, the ones that used to stretch her hands almost in a kind of torture, and played it as if it were the simple C scale. Feeling exhilarated and relaxed at the same time, she stepped away from her piano and admired it for a few more moments before returning to the overstuffed sofa.

"I believe I could sit here all day with a fire in the fireplace and just read!" She said to anyone who was listening.

"There are times when you will do just that. Since we all have known you so well for so long, the books are our gift to you. But there are also many other things for you to see, to learn and ultimately to do while you are here," explained Josef. "Apart from brief periods of rest, you will be kept very busy for a while. That is why we thought you would appreciate this haven to return to for reflection, meditation and relaxation. It is not all work, you know. You must have time for enjoyment and pleasure on a strictly personal level also. However, I know you will find the 'work' pleasurable as well. It is all for spiritual growth, which never stops, no matter where you are."

"For now, I will leave you in the very competent hands of Sarah and Felicia, as I have someone else to greet at this moment. But know that I will come back to you. We are never apart and there is much I have to teach you." With that, Josef wrapped himself in his large wings. He appeared to melt into a glowing golden-white ball of light as he sped away just as you would imagine a flying saucer to do.

CHAPTER 12

"He cuts quite an impressive figure," Christina said to the girls.

"Yes he does. As do all the angels. They are always around us and help us all the time. Their help does not stop just because we left the Earth plane. They are beautiful and have such energy that it is helpful just to be in their presence. When there is a group of them, their energy is felt by all, and the sound of them is still something we look forward to. As a group their voices are heard as music, but music such as you have never heard in the physical. When you hear their magnificence and all you can see is a brilliant light, you know you are in the presence of several Universal beings," answered Felicia.

"Actually, they are normally seen here as a brilliant white-gold light and not in a human form. When they wish to communicate with us they will take a form more familiar or comfortable to us. I guess they think we would feel funny talking to a ball of light," Sarah said with a big grin on her face.

"Now that you brought it up, you two are not angels?" asked Christina.

"No, we are just as you. In fact, if you search your memory back to your grade-school days, you will remember a good friend and classmate that got a case of measles with complications," Felicia told Christina.

"Yes, I remember my friend Janet and not understanding why she had to go and get sick. Most of all I remember my Mother coming to me with the bad news that she had died and gone to heaven. I was young enough not to understand the full impact of what she was saying to me, just that Janet would not be around for me to play with anymore. I believe I was about 9 years old and felt the emptiness of Janet being gone. We would share books, and I taught her to embroider. We made paper-dolls together. After she was gone, I never had a friend to do those kinds of things with again. Of course, I had many, many friends, but it was an exploring kind of friendship that could not be recaptured with someone else," said Christina feeling that old ache returning again, even though she knew Janet was not really "dead."

As she looked at Felicia, she smiled back at Christina and slowly transformed before her into the little blonde pigtailed, freckle-faced, fun-loving Janet of Christina's childhood at 9 years of age.

Christina was dumbstruck! As she stood staring at Felicia all the warm memories and loving feelings came flooding back to her, and even though they were not physical, she felt tears running down her cheeks. The connection to that time in her life was so strong and her love of Janet so strong, that Christina took on the image of herself at the age of 9. The two little 9-year-old girls stood staring at each other, until Christina could stand it no longer and ran over and hugged "Janet." They both savored the moment.

Both returning to adults, Christina said, "But you don't look like Janet. And you are called Felicia. Why is that?"

"What you see is a culmination of many lifetimes. I have been more than Janet and will be more than what you see here. I am known as Felicia, because that is my soul name. I have chosen to use it here."

"Then I must already know you too," Christina said turning to Sarah. "I know I felt an immediate attachment to you both." Before Christina could finish her thought, Sarah began her changing process. Instead of becoming younger as Felicia did, she became older, shorter and heavier. She developed soft wrinkles and gray wispy hair and was wearing old-fashioned wire spectacles. She held out her grandmotherly hands to Christina.

"You are my grandma! I have the most wonderful childhood memories of the weekends at your house. The weekends with my cousins in your large back yard. My gosh, it seems forever ago!" Christina took her grandmother's hands and pulled her to her and gave her a big hug.

"I was too young when you died to have even thought of thanking you for being the grandmother you were. You let me help you make pie crusts for your scrumptious cherry pie. It was such a happy time on Sunday mornings sitting in your lap while you read the funny papers to my brother and me.

"You also taught me to wile away the hours doing embroidery. I believe I was the very first girl in my class to know how to embroider, thanks to you. I thought it was one of the few times I would ever be the first and best at anything. When you died I missed you so terribly. You were my very first encounter with the death of a family member and it was such a blow to me. By this time I had a better understanding of what death was and suffered the loss on a more personal level. I think I was twelve years old at the time. Once again, it was the end of an era, a major part of my life. And at twelve, I didn't know how to let go of that."

"I know. I was with you throughout the entire ordeal and have been with you ever since. I am well aware of what you went through and how you became stronger as a result of it. If you think back, you were the source of comfort for your brother and your cousins. Even though you say you didn't understand fully, you had an inner knowing that you conveyed to the others. Without you, it would have been much more difficult for them. You being the only girl, had more of the intuitive forces going for you. All the boys felt they had to be strong, although they weren't sure why. You provided the balance that was necessary for them," Sarah explained as she returned to her tall, lithe image. At that moment Christina realized Sarah looked very much like the pic-

tures she had seen of her Grandmother as a young woman.
No wonder she looked familiar in the very beginning.

"I continue to watch over them as well. We were
all a close family and still have strong ties. We have been
together before and will be again. Felicia was your Father
in yet another life. In the last life, she volunteered to be
the daughter of your neighborhood family, knowing her life
would be short and she would still be in contact with you.
The family she was born into was supposed to suffer this
loss as a preparation for the children yet to come. You see,
there are no accidents. Each one of the participants knew
of this in advance of their rebirth. It was a loving act on
Felicia's part and not one she was required to do. Her young
death also played an important role in your acceptance of
my death as your grandmother. So you see all our lives are
interwoven over and over again. We are all bound together
in love," Sarah said in her best grandmotherly voice.

"It's all so incredibly beautiful. It's beyond my wild-
est dreams and yet seems so familiar. I know it to be true and
feel I have always known it to be true. How can that be?"
Christina puzzled.

"You are touching the Source of which you are a part
and where the truth lives and always has. It is part of remembering. It is part of becoming who you are. More and more
you will open to the truth that resides within you. You never
lost it - it was just camouflaged by your physicality. As you
separate yourself from your past life, you will become more
unified with your true nature, and you will know," Felicia
lovingly told her.

An excitement filled Christina and she was anxious
to learn more and more.

"Can we go over to the school so I can see what is
happening and who is there and how it is done?" Christina
couldn't dismiss the anxious tone in her voice. With all

the beauty around her, her impatience seem dismally out of place, but she was having difficulty controlling it.

"Of course, we can go over there now if you want. You do have plenty of time to do all things, so you needn't be in a big hurry to do it all at once. We'll head over that way, so you can look in on what's going on," Sarah said maintaining the patience of a saint.

CHAPTER 13

As they walked over the pathway in the direction of the school, Christina couldn't get over the brilliant colors all around her. One building was of the brick covered with ivy style she was familiar with. Behind it were taller buildings of glass. They seemed to shimmer in the light, emitting many colors reminding her of the prisms she experienced on Earth. The prisms, however, were of more and different colors than she had ever seen before. They were radiant, and ever-changing. It occurred to her that perhaps they were not glass at all, but crystal. She used to hang crystals in her windows to reflect the colors of the aura when the sun hit them. These colors reminded her of that, except they were more vibrant, containing colors she had never seen before and could not possibly describe. The grass was still green, but it was a different green than on Earth. The color seemed alive - it vibrated. There were rich, full trees with birds singing from their tops, also more colorful than on Earth. The trees moved with the birds' songs, almost as though they were swaying in rhythm with the sounds in the air. There were flowers everywhere. On Earth Christina loved surrounding herself with flowers in her yard, on her tables and in her kitchen, but none compared with the ones she saw here.

As they approached the school, Christina was sure she heard her Father's voice. Not wanting to disturb the class she ran up to the windows and looked in. Of course, everyone knew she was there, because they all sensed her vibrations being added to the immediate area. Being new to the whole idea, Christina was unaware of her impact on the group. Felicia and Sarah stood back and watched her exuberance, smiling to each other in understanding.

Christina was terribly embarrassed when she realized the entire classroom was looking at her with a variety of expressions on their faces from tolerance to sheer delight.

Since the damage was already done, she backed away from the window and properly walked through the open door. With an apologetic look to her father, who was leading the class, she took a seat in the very back of the room. Her father nodded to her and continued speaking.

The class was on relationships. All relationships. Not just relationships between people, but relationships of people to all things. And relationships between all things. The relationship of color to sound, of trees to animals, of water to air, math to music, of the sciences to astrology and numerology. Everything is related to everything. There are no separations as all things work together to form the whole. Man only chooses to look at them separately and to see them working independently of each other. When in reality they are not independent, but interdependent.

Making mental note that this was definitely a class she wanted to take, Christina quietly left the room in a more unobtrusive manner than the one in which she arrived. Old habits being hard to break, she found herself tiptoeing outside instead of just willing it, which would have been much quicker and would have avoided the few giggles she heard behind her as she left. When she returned to Sarah and Felicia they were both grinning broadly at her and Sarah was shaking her head as if to say, "you will catch on." Realizing the obvious oversight, Christina started laughing at herself and the two girls joined in until they all became weak.

"I never really thought of heaven as being exciting and fun before. I guess I just pictured people sitting around quietly, meditating or just reflecting. I didn't give much thought to what people would really do here," Christina confessed. "In Sunday school I remember seeing pictures of angels sitting on clouds and playing harps. Even at that tender age I thought that would be pretty boring thing to do all day long."

"One thing we are not, is bored," said Felicia.

"Especially when we have someone like you to entertain us," teased Sarah. They all started laughing again.

Christina noticed even the laughter sounded musical, not as harsh as back on Earth, and every bit as much fun.

"As a matter of practice, close your eyes and picture someplace you would like to be right now. One of your favorite places on Earth, or a fantasy place of your mind," instructed Felicia.

Instantly Christina thought of one of her meditation images that was a combination of many places that she had been or seen, and gave her peace and comfort.

"Now open your eyes," Felicia said.

As Christina opened her eyes she saw "her place" more radiant and more beautiful than she ever imagined it in the physical.

"I wrote a poem about this place and I see now that I didn't do it justice. But then I wrote about my Earthly place, not this one," Christina said with a slight crack in her voice.

"You actually created this place with your thoughts when you were in the physical, and when you wrote that poem. We think you have excellent taste and love it here too," praised Felicia.

Christina looked around her and on her left was a small, cool, clear stream with mossy banks on either side. The opposite side of the stream was thickly wooded. Between Christina and the stream were tall pines with reddish bark spaced several yards apart. The path she was standing on was cushioned with pine needles and their fragrance seemed to fill the air. To her right were patches of wild flowers of every imaginable color also lending their delicate scent to the air. The path seemed to open up into a large sweeping meadow. Quite some distance ahead and crowning the meadow were white-capped mountains. This was indeed the creation of her mind about which she wrote her poem "The Magical Forest."

Sarah asked her to recite it to them, while they were standing here in her creation.

Much to her surprise the words came back to her instantly and with ease.

"I feel as though I'm walking in sunshine,
the many trees around, a deep green.
The flowers in a myriad of colors;
with birds adding music to the scene.

"I sit with my back against a tree
and feel the breeze on my face;
I smell the scent of pine in the air
and marvel at this beautiful place.

"Right next to me is a fresh water stream
azure blue with white rocks throughout.
The banks are covered in rich green moss
with ferns' fiddleheads beginning to sprout.

"The clouds floating in a sky deep blue;
wildflowers each with a scent to share;
mushrooms popping up near the water's edge
and squirrels playing tag without a care.

"The dancing waters produce a bright rainbow,
which forms a bridge from shore to shore,
I believe I could walk across it
and play melodies on the colors galore.

"As I look out across the water
a doe reaches the bank to drink.
She stops and looks straight at me
and we did communicate, I think.

"I believe there must be fairies

hiding behind every tree;
or sitting beneath the mushrooms
watching and studying me.

"I love my magical forest
and I visit there every day.
All I have to do is close my eyes
and my imagination whisks me away."

Both girls applauded her as though she had been putting on a performance, but to Christina's mind she was only remembering. Felicia pointed to one of the mushrooms on the near bank and Christina gasped as she saw a tiny white ball bouncing from mushroom to mushroom.

"What is that?" she asked of Sarah.

"That," Sarah said delightedly, "is one of your fairies. We don't see them too often because they are so tiny and move so quickly. Plus they like to tease and play games. Just as you think you see one, they simply disappear. Their primary function is to take care of the plant life on Earth, large and small, and they are part of the angelic kingdom. As they slow down you can see their beautiful angelic shape, if they want you to, of course."

With that the tiny light stopped for a second and Christina did see a little figure with delicate wings, before it became a speck of light headed in the direction of the wildflowers. It reminded Christina of the way hummingbirds would stop for a second and then dart away barely visible.

"Even though we always heard about fairies when growing up, I never gave much thought to them being real. It seemed as though they belonged in a fairy tale instead," Christina thought out loud.

"One of the well kept secrets. Yes, they are real and are a very important part of Earth life. They are the guardians of your forests and gardens and mankind should be very grateful for them. We think the reason for their being generally unknown on Earth is for the reason you described. They belong in fairy tales, and of course adults don't believe in fairy tales. And it would be too embarrassing for a mature individual to admit to believing in fairies. Those people that do have knowledge of them and who work with them have the most beautiful and flourishing gardens. People should call on them to help with their flowers, plants, bushes and trees. Anything growing from the soil could be enhanced if people would call on the fairies for their help. They are not imaginary, but very real, seen or not," explained Felicia.

"What an exciting discovery!" Christina was just overwhelmed at actually being in "her" place and at seeing a real fairy.

"Having written about them, I guess my inner Self knew even if my physical self did not. I just did not know that I knew," Christina said with a new awareness.

"What about animals? Are they here? Is this where they come too?" Christina asked suddenly aware of this large oversight, since animals had always been so important to her.

"Of course they are here," Sarah answered with amusement.

"But I haven't seen any."

"Because the subject had not come up and you have been very busy with many other discoveries. You are rushing again instead of taking the time to enjoy each new experience," Felicia said exhibiting her supreme, gentle patience, once again.

Realizing this before Felicia even spoke it, Christina apologized for her impatience and said, "I must be a trying experience for you two."

"Not at all. And you need not apologize, for it is all part of the learning process and new discoveries, no matter where you are, it can cause a certain amount of impatience.

You will slow down before long, once you become more familiar with how things work here, and once you realize you have lots and lots of time before you have to go anywhere. We love you and we don't have anywhere else to go either," said Felicia as she put her arms around Christina and gave her a big hug.

CHAPTER 14

"Were you thinking of any one animal in particular?" Asked Sarah.

"Well, yes I guess I was. I was thinking of my dog Cookie who was just a mutt and my Siamese cat Ling. There were many others over the years that I would love to see, but those two were extra special, I suppose," Christina said with a far-off look in her eyes.

"By now you should know what to do, huh?" Reminded Felicia.

With a big grin, Christina said, "I guess I should, huh?" She closed here eyes and pictured Cookie and Ling and when she opened them, coming down the path from the direction of the meadow far in the distance, she could see two small figures heading her way. She could feel the anticipation creating a heart-like feeling in her chest, like a child coming downstairs early on Christmas morning. She stood and watched as the two small figures became larger and larger. She could see a tail wagging and a smile on Cookie's face with her tongue hanging out. Ling was directly by Cookie's side and was matching Cookie's stride, step for step. Without even hesitating, Cookie reached Christina and jumped up putting her two front paws on Christina's thighs. Christina scratched behind her floppy ears and nuzzled her face kissing her soft nose as she used to. She then bent over and picked up Ling and holding him like a baby ran her hand along his long back to the tip of his tail. He naturally responded by purring as he always did. She spoke lovingly and softly to him and he continued purring, closing his eyes in sheer bliss.

"Isn't it funny even though you know what you know, you don't think you will ever see them again when they leave you?" Christina asked with a dumbfounded expression on her face.

"We know how you feel all too well. Remember, we were where you are now with our own instructors and discoveries and realizations. You ask yourself how you could have felt that way or how you could have believed that, once you realize the Divine Plan for all things created. It is all so very simple. It is all based on love. The love is never diminished or gone, but can only be enhanced. We are never separated from those we love. Even our pets," Sarah related.

"We help animals grow and evolve through our love for them," explained Felicia.

Our love separates them from their group and elevates them to a level of receiving and giving love. Once we love them, they are always with us. See?"

At her last question, Christina looked away from Ling and toward Felicia to see a large German Shepherd with soft, brown eyes standing by her side. He looked up at Felicia and his love for her was purely visible. She returned the look and he settled down at her feet.

The thought that Sarah and Felicia had pets never occurred to Christina and she again felt ashamed at having been so selfishly single-minded.

"Let it go. It is natural. Remember, we have all been there. As beautiful as this place is, we should be going. There is more to see and we can't stay here forever," Felicia said jokingly.

With that the German Shepherd, Ling and Cookie got up together and started off down the path toward the meadow. Halfway there, all three stopped and turned and looked at the three girls, as if to say, "See ya later!"

Looking at her magical forest one more time, listening to the waters of the stream and enjoying the fresh aroma of the pine trees and flowers, Christina turned to leave. Felicia and Sarah each took one of Christina's hands and they soared above it all, returning to Christina's cottage.

"We think you have had enough experiences for the moment and it is time for you to rest and reflect on what you have seen. When you feel you have sufficiently rested, send us a thought and we will be back to get you for your next adventure," Felicia suggested.

Christina realized she would love to sit in her new living room and read for a short time, and it surely wouldn't hurt to go over in her mind some of the past activities. "I have been busy," she thought.

CHAPTER 15

Even though she knew no one was in her house, she could not resist the inclination to use the angel knocker on her front door. She took hold of the angel and rapped two times and the front door swung open for her. This tickled her so much she walked into her room and started giggling which accelerated into full-fledged laughter as she fell down on her overstuffed sofa thinking "This is just like 'Open Sesame' when I was a child! The magic door-knocker!"

Once snuggled down in her sofa, she was glad she was there and relaxing. She went over her new experiences, which had been many. Remembering, remembering. She thought of Bill and the girls and wanted to be with them again, but refrained from letting the will take over. She thought about Josef and his magnificent stature and realized she had intuitively known about him on Earth. He was the one she talked to when she had a problem to be solved, or when she was sad and needed a special friend. She just had not put a face or figure to him and had not even thought about him being an angel. He was just someone she talked to mentally.

She then thought about her Mother and Father and the loving warmth they gave her, that she had missed for so long. The parental love that is so much a part of your life while growing up. The parental love you never expect to be without on Earth. The parental love that saw you through all your trials and errors. The parental love that was unconditional. The shock you go through when they leave you. The love is still there, but is not the same somehow. It is no longer tangible. You hurt with the inability to touch, to hold. It was missed.

Her brother. She still had not seen him and she wondered where he was and what he was doing. "I hope I see him soon," she wished.

She thought about Janet and her Grandmother, and how stunned she was by the fact they were Sarah and Felicia. Reflecting on this, she now knew that she knew. She remembered how she felt connected to them both when she "first" met them. "To feel this connection, I must have known, I just didn't realize it yet," she said to no one in particular.

She marveled at the ability to visualize and create so easily. Looking around her room she felt so peaceful here. She remembered her first experience at creating the apple and thinking that would be really tasty about now, and held out her hand and closed her eyes. The apple graciously appeared in her palm.

She could smell the sweetness of it and bit into it, not at all surprised at its juicy, crispness and taste which surpassed any apples ever eaten in the physical.

She got up, pulled down a book from her shelves, and settled down on the window seat to look out on the vibrantly colored garden before opening her book. She disappeared into her book for quite some time and was feeling quite rested. She then put the book down and walked around the room just "feeling" it. It seemed alive somehow. Anything could be changed at any time and maybe this is what made it seem alive. It was forever moving, not solid. It occurred to her that it was the same on Earth. We just viewed everything as solid, but everything is made of energy, therefore the atomic particles and molecules are constantly moving and not solid at all.

In reviewing her experiences since her arrival, she realized how much she had discovered, remembered and just generally been through. It should have been exhausting, but instead she felt revitalized, renewed and anxious to learn more.

CHAPTER 16

Deciding she was well-rested, Christina sent thoughts to the girls who immediately appeared at her open front door, all smiles.

"You are looking wonderful and happy, Christina," Felicia complimented. "We may not be physical, but we need to collect and heal the energies that were associated with the physical, particularly in illness. You appear to have done that quite well with your rest."

"Do you remember us telling you there were several levels of existence here? That you could move to the levels lower than yours, but not higher?" Sarah asked.

Christina, remembering, nodded.

"We think it is time to visit some of these places. Are you ready?"

Christina nodded again, but was not overly anxious, nor was she sure she was ready. Believing herself to be ready for more learning just moments ago, she was afraid this would be more than she bargained for.

"There is nothing to fear and we will be by your side at all times. No matter what you see you must remember these people can improve their situation at any time. If they appear to be stuck where they are, it is by their own choice," indicated Felicia.

The girls each took one of Christina's hands and they took flight. At first Christina felt as if they were descending, however, realized it was more a lateral flight than a downward motion. The scenery below changed and although beautiful was not the same as where they had just left.

The three gently touched down and Felicia and Sarah let go of Christina's hands. Christina looked around and noticed some differences. First and most obvious was the lack of the Angelic voices in the air. Next the colors, although still more beautiful than on Earth, did not have the same vibrancy as her place. She walked over to the nearest tree and laid her hand on the bark expecting to hear the same sounds she heard at home. She was disappointed when the sounds, although audible, were not as clear and did not produce the same vibrations within her. It made her think of someone putting a handkerchief over the mouthpiece of a telephone to change or dull the voice, giving it a muted quality.

However, as she touched the flowers they still responded as her own did. It was so nearly the same here, that if you had not been to her place, this would indeed be heaven to those residing here.

As she looked around at the homes and the buildings, they were exceptional, but still lacking to her mind. She noticed a large white building and intuitively knew this to be the school. There was a group of people standing outside the building talking among themselves, and appeared to be waiting to enter the classrooms. Within the group she noticed a young couple with two children, a boy and a girl perhaps 6 and 8 years of age, respectively. The young couple, obviously the parents, was engaged in a conversation with another, very good-looking young man with black curly hair.

"Come," said Sarah, "there are some people we want you to meet."

As they approached the group, Felicia greeted the young couple and turned to Christina, "I would like you to meet Maria and her Earth husband Walter. These are their two children Jeffrey and Harriett." She then turned to the young man with the black curly hair and said, "And this is Gregory."

Christina nodded to each in turn, tousled Jeffrey's hair and smiling said, "It is very nice to meet you." Not knowing what else to say, or why she had been introduced to them, she blurted out, "Have you been here long?"

Walter laughed and said, "Been here long waiting for class, or been here long?" As he stretched out his
arm and made a complete circle as though presenting the
whole world.

Already well aware of how ridiculous her question
sounded and wanting to take it all back, she responded, "It
really was a stupid question, and the answer is also really
none of my business. I'm sorry."

This time Maria laughed, "There is nothing at all to
apologize for and as far as I am concerned there is no such
thing as a stupid question. I am sure you know there is no
such thing as time so it is all relative, I suppose."

Felicia offered, "We wanted you to meet Maria and
Walter and hear their story. We found it extraordinary and
thought you would too. They all have been working very
hard and will be joining us very soon. We thought you could
be part of the welcoming committee when they arrive."

Christina was very pleased to be thought of in this
way and said, "I would be very happy to be there when you
arrive. Please tell me your story."

Maria began, "Every Thanksgiving our family and
my brother's and sister's families would spend the day at our
Mother's home. We would all pitch in and help with dinner
and the clean up, but it was getting to be too much for her so
this was to be our last one together at her house. Thereafter
we would share in the responsibilities, alternating between
our homes. As a tribute to our Mother for all the wonderful
Thanksgivings and to celebrate the end of an era, we had all
decided to chip in and buy her a gift of a painting she had always wanted. It was my job to pick it up and wrap it, which
I did.

"It was early afternoon when we left home and headed for Mother's. The traffic was terrible, the children were
in the back seat, and Walter and I were discussing what it
would be like to live in a small town and not have to put up

with this kind of holiday traffic. We talked about small towns more and more frequently, while never actually admitting that the thought of moving to one was in the back of our minds.

"The kids were singing in the back seat and Walter and I had just exchanged one of those 'Isn't it great?' looks at one another that lasted all of one second. As we both returned our gaze out the windshield we saw a car on the other side of the freeway suddenly careen out of control, jump the median strip and aim directly at us. Before Walter could think or react, the car hit us head on. It was so sudden I didn't feel a thing. In a matter of seconds it was over and I looked at myself amazed that I was all in one piece. I looked over and saw Walter draped over the wheel. I then checked the back seat and the two children appeared as two little rag dolls crumpled together as though sleeping.

"In a state of panic I leaned over the back of my seat to get to the children, but was unable to grip them or help them. As I turned to return to my sitting position to help Walter, I saw my body slumped over toward Walter as though trying to reach for him. It was then that I knew I had not survived the crash. I went around the car to Walter's side and as I approached I saw Walter leaving his body. Seeing me, he also knew what had happened. Now our only concern was for the children and how we could help them. As I had done, Walter reached out for them, but was unable to make contact as he saw his hand pass through them."

Walter spoke up and said, "I turned to Maria and asked what can we do? We have got to help them. We have to find help. Admittedly I was in a frantic state and yelled to no one in particular, 'Please help us!'

"A figure appeared between our two children holding their hands. I couldn't tell if it was male or female, but it said, 'Your children are fine and with me.'"

"I knew then that they were still with us, even if not among the living," Maria continued. Walter then went over to the driver of the car that had hit us and turned to me and shook his head. He came back and told me that evidently in the spirit of the holiday, the driver had been drinking. I didn't even ask him how he knew this. I just accepted it to be true.

"It was at that moment what we believed to be an angelic presence with our children motioned to us to follow it. Without the least bit of hesitation, we did. With it just ahead of us still holding our children's hands we entered a tunnel of golden-white light which led us here. We saw our families that had gone before us within the tunnel, smiling, greeting, and sending love. There were many of our friends there as well. I marveled at the joy I felt and the total lack of pain considering what we had been through. It was all so quick we were spared that.

"We were greeted by many other beautiful people who helped us with our adjustment, in what appeared to be a kind of hospital room. They cared for us, talked to us and encouraged us to rest. Besides the four of us there were others in the room and among them was Gregory. We have remained together since then because of a very strong connection that began many lifetimes ago, although we did not know him in our most recent one. That is, not until the accident. He was the driver of the other car."

Christina felt a big intake of what would be termed as breath in the physical. Although not actually breathing, it sure felt the same.

Maria continued, "It was all part of the plan for each of us. Experiences. That is what it is all about. We have learned this through our classes here. The hard part for us was feeling what our families were going through back on Earth. And I actually felt awful about the picture in the trunk of the car being destroyed, when Mother would have enjoyed it so. But again, we have learned this was an experience each one of us chose to go through for our own personal growth.

"The children are finishing out their lessons as children by their own choice. Even though they are here, they can still experience what would have been their childhood. Once completed they will take the young adult form that most suits them. We know now they are not 'our' children, but old souls just as ourselves, and we all chose to be together as a family as we have many times before."

Gregory spoke for the first time, "You see, I have been part of their family before.

I was planning a rest from physical experience, but instead elected to act as a catalyst for the events Maria related. I was at rest in the physical because, ridiculous as it may sound, the accident was my purpose. I created the accident when I was only 17 years of age, having accomplished little else to that point. By divine design others were naturally affected also: my Mother in that life; Maria's family; Walter's family; the children's friends and classmates; my friends and classmates; and there was no mistake in that. I am sure you have heard the expression, 'there is no such thing as an accident.'"

Felicia hastened to add, "That is not to say there is no free will, because there is. There are just some circumstances that fall within the realm of Karma, which is the law of cause and effect, or action and reaction, or debtor and debtee. It would be necessary to go back several lifetimes to see the entire picture, but it is safe to say that lots of debts were satisfied, by all parties involved."

Christina turned to Maria, Walter and Gregory, "Thank you for sharing your story with me. It has certainly opened my eyes. I see you all together and can see the tremendous bond. It has been my pleasure to have been allowed to share in your story. I have enjoyed meeting you and look forward to greeting you all at my home very soon."

She bent down and hugged toe-headed Jeffrey and then Harriett with a twinkle in her eyes.

"We look forward to it too," said Walter.

The three girls turned to leave and Christina turned back for a last look at her new friends, in time to see Harriett reach out and pulled on Jeffrey's ear just enough to make him squeal a little. They all disappeared into the school.

"That was quite a story and I must admit at first I was shocked they were friends with the man who killed them. But then I realized how silly that was, because they were not killed at all. He didn't really hurt them, he just cut their Earth visit short," Christina confessed.

"We knew you would see it that way," said Sarah.

"But I didn't at first," Christina said feeling a little ashamed.

"But you did come to a full understanding and acceptance quickly, without allowing yourself to judge," said Sarah.

"Are you ready for your next adventure?" asked Felicia.

"I suppose I am," Christina answered hesitantly.

CHAPTER 17

As before Felicia and Sarah each took one of Christina's hand and they took off. Christina swore she could feel the air change around her as they landed. She immediately noticed the difference in her surroundings. The layout was basically the same with the houses and a school, but the houses were simple, a few being somewhat crude in appearance. The colors of the trees, flowers and grass were washed out. And there was even a very slight dampness in the air. It was not exactly un-pleasant, it was just not as pleasant as her place.

As they wandered around Christina noticed the residents here were not quite as joyful and smiling as in the other places. You would hear occasional laughter or see an occasional smile but it was not as predominant. She also noticed the lack of celestial music. Closing her eyes and concentrating on listening for music, she was able to pick out a few notes and voices, but as soon as she opened her eyes and lost her concentration, they disappeared.

"As you can see there is a definite difference between the levels," commented Sarah.

"Yes I did notice. What level is this anyway?" Christina asked.

"What level it is, is unimportant. What you are seeing and learning is. There is no room for judgment here or anywhere else for that matter. Remember... we are all exactly where we are supposed to be at all times. And that is true both here and on the Earth plane," said Felicia as she hugged herself against the damper surroundings.

Sarah spoke up with a suggestion, "Why don't we surround ourselves with warm light to protect ourselves from the cooler dampness?"

"Good thought, Sarah," said Felicia as she reached out for her and Christina's hands.

The three girls held hands in a small circle and Sarah instructed, "We will begin by imagining. Create a ball of light around yourself. Within that ball is a gentle warmth which coats you like a woolen sweater while drying the air immediately around you."

As Christina visualized her ball, she instantly felt better. And it did indeed feel as though she was wearing her favorite wool sweater.

"You could have visualized an actual sweater instead of the ball of light, which would have made you comfortable against the cooler surroundings, but the ball also serves the purpose of an insulator against any negative vibrations that would possibly be sent your way, or that may just be generated in an area near or around you.

"It is not that someone would deliberately try to harm you. But it is a fact that some of the people here have various negative issues they are working on and not realizing the power of such thoughts or vibrations, would not try to control them in your presence.

These vibrations do have a definite impact on us. We can still feel them, but in our protective state they will not penetrate our being. The best we can do for them is to counter their negativity by sending them love. This also helps them to resolve their issues and to move on more quickly," Felicia explained.

"Come on, we have someone we want you to meet," said Sarah as she ran ahead toward a very small cottage that looked as though it needed a little TLC.

As they approached behind Sarah, Christina stopped to enjoy the flowers bordering the walkway. Although not as vibrant as her own, they still had a beauty to be enjoyed. They looked well cared for.

Sarah skipped up to the door with hand raised to knock, when a voice said, "Don't bother Sarah dear, just come on in. All of you. And welcome. It is so nice to see you again and your new friend Christina. Welcome to you too, dear."

The fact that this 'voice' knew her, startled Christina.

The voice was coming from a very small, old lady with gray hair piled in a top-knot on top of her head. The wrinkles in her face delicately sculpted a smile which was complimented by dancing blue eyes.

"Please sit down." The room was sparsely furnished, but comfortable. There was a fire in the fireplace next to the old lady in the rocking chair.

It occurred to Christina that this was the first "old" person she had seen since arriving here.

Christina thought to herself, "Hadn't the girls told me that people took the form that was the most comfortable or natural for them? Usually as a young adult. Maybe being old was the most comfortable for this woman."

"My name is Angela, and I am here to help the residents. I took this form because old is usually associated with wisdom. People are less intimidated by older people and often turn to them for help and advice. Anything I can do to help these souls move onward and upward, so to speak, is what I am here to do," Angela said in answer to Christina's thoughts.

"I am sorry. I still haven't learned how to shelter my thoughts from others. I did not intend to insult or offend you. I have much to learn also. Please forgive my thoughtlessness, or should I say thoughts," Christina apologized.

"My dear, no offense was taken and I truly understand. All of your thoughts came from your heart and were honest. You were not entertaining one thought of hurtful or inconsiderate intent. Please don't apologize," Angela said trying to calm Christina.

"Have you told her anything about the situation here?" Angela asked the girls.

Both girls shook their head in response. Christina looked from one to another with a big question mark in the middle of her forehead.

"Angela is here by choice. It is her desire to help everyone get past their current belief systems and negativism, that are holding them here," explained Felicia.

"Isn't there a school here too?" Christina asked with a little concern.

"Yes, there are schools for those that wish to attend, but often it takes the residents a long time to make that choice, because they believe this is all there is and that they already know it all. Unfortunately, if you already know it all, what would be the point in going to school? We brought you here to meet Angela, who is an Angel," offered Felicia in a voice that almost sounded like a whisper.

"The residents come to me to talk. I am the wise old lady who has 'been around.' Rarely do people go to someone younger than themselves for help and advice. And they certainly wouldn't go to someone outfitted in white robes and wings! And since they all feel they are in the same boat together, who can they turn to? Of course their angels are always with them also, but they are not geared to see them or accept them. Until they do, their angels can only watch over them and pray for them, which they have done since the beginning. Their impact can be felt in only the most subtle of ways until the souls become more aware of who they themselves are and where they are going. That is where I come in. I try to convince them that this place is not the 'be all to end all.' That there is so much more to themselves than what they currently know; that they need to attend the school that is here just for them. If not needed, why is it here? I keep busy," Angela added.

"You see Christina, no matter what you see, or how poor the situation may seem, no one is ever left alone or without help and guidance. This fact should not be forgotten as we move to the next levels," cautioned Sarah.

As Christina looked at Angela who was smiling at her, she realized the depth of those blue eyes and felt she could disappear into them, which generated a great feeling of comfort within her. Now she understood the power Angela had to guide and direct these people who came to her.

"Thank you Angela, for explaining the circumstances here and helping me to understand and also for being patient with me. There is so much for me to learn, but what you are doing is so important I don't want to take up so much of your time." Christina said.

"What is time?" Angela answered, and as she did, her blue eyes became slits among the soft folds of skin surrounding them and she laughed. When she laughed, Christina heard that wonderful angelic music, voices in song and chimes. It was loud and clear and uplifting.

Watching Angela, Christina was taken with her good nature and quick smile and obvious sense of humor in spite of the dreary surroundings. Just being with her made Christina feel this place wasn't really so awful after all.

The three girls got up to leave and Angela rose to hug each one. No one said a word. As they were walking away from the cottage, Christina turned and looked back at the doorway where Angela had been standing and in her place she saw a small globe of golden-white light gently bouncing back and forth. Before turning away, she saw the globe melt into a tall slender form with blonde hair, dancing blue eyes, and wings reaching the floor. The image lasted what would be a split second in Earth-time and as Christina waved, a little old lady with gray hair on top of her head waved back.

CHAPTER 18

"That was really great!" Christina said to the girls.

"We knew you would enjoy Angela. We wanted to show you that no one is ever alone," said Felicia.

"Are you ready to go on?" Asked Sarah.

"No, I don't think so," said Christina. "I think I would like to return to my own cottage and assimilate what I've seen and heard so far. Is there a chance I could check on Bill and the girls? Then I should be ready to continue."

"Very well, we will return home. We will call on Josef for your return to Earth," Felicia said.

All three held hands and Christina again felt motion before gently touching the ground in front of her personal haven. The colors were almost blinding at first. The richness was overwhelming, the fragrance 'heavenly,' as well as the sounds. Being in the other level had caused her to lose touch with the beauty here almost as though she had forgotten. It was good to be home.

Felicia and Sarah bid her a temporary farewell and left her. She just stood and admired the flowers bordering her walkway, comparing them to those at Angela's. She must miss these brilliant colors, the warmth, and everything about this place, she found herself thinking.

"Never, Christina my dear. You see, I can be in more than one place at a time. There is nothing to miss."

Christina, startled, turned in all directions looking for the musical voice she knew to be Angela's. She did not see her anywhere. She slowly walked toward her door, still admiring her flowers. When she put her hand on the knob, she looked back at her walkway just in time to see a golden-white globe speed away.

She entered her living room glad for the warm feeling she got from it. Smiling, she headed for her overstuffed sofa. Her thought was to 'flop' into it, but knowing she had no physical form this would be difficult. Flopping took weight. This task was going to take a bit of concentration. She edged over to the sofa and closed her non-physical eyes and visualized herself kicking both feet up and becoming heavy and airborne to land in, rather than on, the sofa. At that instant she kicked up both feet. Down she came, landing definitely 'in' the sofa. She was 'in' so far she could not see out. She was within the sofa. "Guess this is going to take more practice," she thought as she visualized herself standing next to the sofa. Up she came to a standing position. "Do I want to try that again?"

Deciding in the positive, she again kicked up her feet. She felt the sofa gently fold around her as she made a perfect three-point landing.

"Definitely worth it," she said to herself as she settled in to review in her mind the events of her travels.

CHAPTER 19

Relaxed and comfortable in her haven, Christina began reviewing her recent adventures. She thought about the first experience with Maria. She liked them all. And to her own surprise she really liked Gregory. She wondered what their reaction would be to this place when they arrived, and what the children would look like. Would they be all grown? Will they have taken their adult form before they get here? Will they all arrive together as a group? Will that all depend on what they learn at school? She didn't know she had so many questions. She had Felicia and Sarah....who was going to be their guide or guides?

In her mind she moved on to the next level and Angela. "How awful it must be to live there in that dampness and lackluster environment," she thought. Then it occurred to her that they didn't know it to be awful. It was all they knew. They had no comparison. She did. "Maybe it seems beautiful to them. If that is the case, what is beyond me? Does this place seem lackluster to others? Is there something more beautiful beyond here?" She questioned and questioned until she actually felt weary.

She got up to get a book to get away from all the questions and returned to her sofa. This time she decided to forego the 'flopping' routine. She settled in to read for awhile. Since there is no time, she didn't know how long she had read, but she managed to complete three chapters when she heard a gentle rap on her door. Testing her own powers, she reached out mentally to see who was there. She knew immediately that it was Josef.

"Come in please, Josef."

"Very good Christina. You are a quick study, I see," replied Josef.

"Just thought I would try it and see if it worked," Christina admitted. "Everyone seems to know what I am thinking before I say it, who I am before I enter their house, so I thought I'd try it myself."

"Well done. I understand you want to return to your husband and daughters. Are you sure? You will have to learn to separate yourself from their emotions and not become entangled. I don't think you want to repeat your last experience," Josef cautioned.

"I know, and you are right, I don't. But you said you would teach me and I really must see how they are doing," she replied.

"Already you are becoming anxious. You must gain control first. And yes, I will teach you."

"Can we start now? I mean, right now?"

"Yes, my dear. Right now. Gaining control comes with knowledge. There are things you must know and understand. I know your great love for your family and the strain of being separated from them. This is your starting point. You are remembering and feeling the Earthly love. That is a protective and possessive love. They were your family. But I did say, were. Of course, there are strong ties from being together many, many times before and many times again. But individual families are an Earth condition. Here we are all interconnected and one. Yes, you and Bill are soul mates and will be together. Everything your family is experiencing is purely physical and temporary. As you now know, in reality nothing can hurt or harm them. It is simply a fleeting experience by which they learn valuable lessons or insights. You know they don't belong to you. They are not your family. However, I can appreciate your concerns. I also know these feelings cannot be shut off just because you are no long on the Earth plane. Just remember that no matter what they are going through now, you will all be together again."

"Okay. I guess I never thought of it all that way. Some of it I knew and some of it I just did not want to accept. But how do I let go? I don't know if I am capable of that."

"But you are. Stop looking at them as their personalities, but see them as who they really are. All of you are souls on a path to Cosmic Consciousness. The whole picture is so much greater than what you are allowing yourself to see. You are concentrating on one grain of sand and overlooking the entire beach. Each member of your family is in truth an old soul seeking the same things as you.

"This realization is the first step in your protection. It will protect you from the emotions being put out into the ethers that can trap you. The second is concentration. You must concentrate on your desire. Whether that desire is to be of help to your family or to return 'home,' it all works in the same way. The third is, as I said, desire. And last, and most certainly not least, you must remember I am always with you. Just ask and I am there, as it has always been.

"Now, if you are ready, I will stay by your side for your first return visit."

"Yes. I am definitely ready. I am just glad you are there."

"Then let's be off!"

As quickly as a bolt of lightning they transported to Christina's old living room, where Bill was sitting in his chair. Christina thought he looked so much older.
She turned to Josef and opened her mouth to speak, but before she could he stopped her.

"Remember...just call me," said Josef as he gave Christina a flamboyant bow, a wink, a smile, and he was gone.

With a feeling of slight trepidation for what she had embarked upon, Christina had to hold back the urge to call Josef right back. She looked at Bill, and he really did look older.

"Boy, what a number grief will do on you! Bill actually has a few more gray hairs, and a least a couple more worry lines. But I must say he does not look as depressed as before, just tired."

Bill was actually dozing in his chair waiting for the oven buzzer to go off indicating his gourmet TV dinner was ready. He never was one to go in for cooking. Christina was always so good at just throwing something together in a hurry that tasted as though she had given it a lot of thought and work. He was not above helping her with the chopping and peeling or even setting the table and he was great at taking orders. Planning a menu was a bigger job than he had ever wanted to tackle in the kitchen. Thank heaven for TV dinners and cans.

The buzzer sounded and Bill awoke and rubbed his eyes and stretched a little before getting out of his chair. There was no fire in the fireplace so Christina figured it must be late spring or even summer. She followed Bill as he made his way to the kitchen and she thought he was moving a little more slowly than he used to. She stopped in the doorway to watch him.

"What a difference! What's going on here anyway?" she said aloud to the air around her. At that point, Tippy, who had been sleeping under the kitchen table, jumped up and ran over to her wagging his tail.

"What is it boy? What do you see there?" Bill asked him as he reached down and scratched his ears. Tippy continued wagging his tail at the doorway.

"Christina? Is that you? Are you here?" he asked, feeling a little foolish.

"Oh, it is me, Bill! How I wish you could hear me. But I will tell you all about it tonight when you go to sleep."

Tippy lay down at her feet, but to Bill it was right in the middle of the doorway. "Tippy boy, you are going to have to move before I trip over you. Why on earth would you lie there anyway?"

Bill pulled his dinner from the oven and carried it over to the table to the place he has set for himself. He stared at it for a minute and told Tippy, "I sure do miss the good old days and the good old dinners and the good old conversations with Christina. Do you want to hear how my day was? Well, classes went well, but a lot of students were out with the summer flu. But there were more interactions because of the smaller classes and I really did like that. I have often thought it would be nice to teach younger students in a private school that has smaller classes. One of these days I just may do that. I think I am getting ripe for a change. Everything I am doing now is what I was doing when Christina was with me and it creates a loneliness that I can't say I am particularly fond of."

Tippy wagged his tail in agreement and looked at Christina then back at Bill as if to say, "She's right here. Can't you see her?"

Finishing his dinner, Bill got up and threw away his TV dinner tray, washed his silverware and filled a cup with coffee and carried it with him to the living room to read a while before going to bed. For some reason he was finding it difficult to concentrate on his book and kept looking around the room as if expecting someone. He decided he did not feel alone tonight and it wasn't Tippy taking up the extra space, it was something or someone else.

"If you are here with me tonight Christina, could you please give me some kind of sign?"

Christina looked around the room for something she might be able to move or knock off a table. Something!

She then remembered hearing stories about people using the power of their minds to move objects in the physical world. If it could be done there, certainly she could do it from here where everything seemed so much simpler and matter of fact. Energy, she thought. "That's it! Electrical energy! Why not try to turn a light on or off? If all things are energy, it should be fairly simple. If I concentrate on that lamp across the room maybe I can turn it on."

She planted her feet apart and placed her hands on her hips and bending slightly at the waist, as if this would help, and stared at the lamp across from Bill, willing it turn on. The lamp staunchly and elegantly stood on the table in its darkened state. No illumination here. Reasserting herself, Christina leaned back and thrust herself forward at the waist once more, only this time with a more determined look resembling a scowl and started willing. As if in defiance, the lamp sat steadfastly in the off mode.

"Maybe I should be trying a lamp that is already on and turn it off," she said to herself. "For some reason turning it off seems simpler."

Determined to make herself known to Bill, she headed toward his reading lamp. Concentrating with every ounce of strength she had she visualized Bill's light going out. She tried to see the electrical energy as a physical substance. Suddenly the light flickered slightly, but did not go out.

"Must be a power surge, right Tippy?" Tippy whined a wagged his tail at Christina as if to say she was on the right track.

With her newfound power, Christina managed another flicker for Bill's benefit and at the same moment Tippy stood up and faced Christina and acknowledged her success with his swiftly moving tail. Bill caught the whole episode out of the corner of his eye and began doubting the power surge explanation.

"Christina?"

"Wow, I did it!" Once more she caused a flicker of the light. "But this is taking a lot more of my energy than I expected. If I was capable of feeling tired, I would. Yes, Bill I am here!"

Bill knew now for certain there was more than Tippy and himself in that room. He felt the presence of his beloved Christina. She always did light up a room when she entered! "Christina, I know you are here and I had hoped all

along that somehow you would be able to make your presence known to me. With practice on both our parts maybe
we can perfect this procedure and actually communicate. I
have missed you so terribly. Even after all this time, I have
never stopped missing you."

"After all this time? I just got here. What does he
mean, 'After all this time'? Granted a few months have
passed, because it is no longer winter here." She floated
over to a stack of papers on the fireplace hearth and tried to
read the date. Tippy's eyes followed her every movement
and Bill was watching him watch her.

"What's she doing, boy?'

Tippy got up from his spot at Bill's feet and went
over to Christina in front of the fireplace. Christina bent
over and talked sweetly to him and he responded with his
tail once more. All this was certainly not wasted on Bill,
who instantly knew Christina was talking to Tippy. Christina patted the stack of papers and Tippy obediently stood
up with his front paws resting on the papers, waiting for her
to scratch his ears. She reached down to him and mentally
scratched his ears and he responded by lifting he nose to her
and closing his eyes. Bill was immediately aware of what
was happening and watched the scene in a state of disbelief.

"Even though I see what is happening here, I still
find it hard to believe. Tippy sees you perfectly and is react-
ing to your attentions. Why in the world can't I? I am sure
I want to see you more than he does." With that Bill closed
his eyes and tried to will Christina to appear before him. He
squeezed his eyes tightly, which caused him to screw up his
entire face, pursing his lips and furrowing his brow, making Christina laugh. Reminded her of when the girls, during
one of their spats, would make what they thought were scary
faces at each other.

Christina smiled at Tippy and said "Tell him he is
trying too hard! He just needs to relax and go with it."

Tippy cocked his head and looked at her as if he almost understood what she was saying. He dropped to the floor and ran over to Bill and placed his front paws on Bill's leg and looked right into his eyes as if to convey Christina's message. Bill saw an almost pleading look in Tippy's eyes.

"She said something to you, didn't she boy? Are you trying to tell me something?"

Tippy jumped down and wagging his tail furiously, looked back and forth from Christina to Bill.

"If I can't see or talk to Christina, I guess I am going to have to learn dog-talk and let you be the interpreter, hey boy?" Tippy appeared agreeable to that suggestion, loving all the attention he was getting.

Christina, remembering her goal of finding a date somewhere just before she got sidetracked, started for Bill's desk sitting back out of the way in the corner of the room. As she floated over there, Tippy followed. She wasn't sure if Bill had been tearing off the pages of his Day-At-A-Time calendar, but it would be close enough. "My gosh, no wonder he is looking a little grayer around the temples! But I've only been gone a few days or maybe a month! This calendar says it is June of 1996, which means I have been gone two years already. That is impossible!" Christina started floating back and forth as if pacing, in an agitated state. This in turn started to upset Tippy who started running and jumping back and forth with her.

Bill, noticing Tippy's odd behavior, called out to Christina. "What's wrong sweetheart? Is something wrong? Are you okay? Tell me...talk to me...PLEASE!"

Her strong desire to quickly put Bill at ease and let him know she was all right, allowed her to very briefly materialize in front of, and just above him. She looked down at herself and she was actually glowing in this density and she could see right through herself.

"This is really weird," she thought to herself.

"Weird is not the word for it," Bill responded. As he reached for her, the image was gone. "I knew it! I knew it. She was here all along! Are you still here? Tippy, is she still here? I not only saw her, but I heard her too." He was practically shouting.

"He heard me, and saw me," Christina said aloud, but this time only heard by Tippy. "It may have been short-lived, no pun intended, but I made it through to him. But at least, now he knows I am here with him and that is what I came to do. Perhaps with more practice, I can keep the physical image longer. But I wonder how? I am not really sure how I did it that time. Speaking of time - how could two years have passed and I not know it? I was busy, but not that busy. It seems as though I have not accomplished much at all, if it has been two years. I am going to have to ask some questions when I get back.

"Now I have to go back over what happened and figure out how I did that. Let's see. I was upset. Would that have done it? No I don't think so. Was it just a freak accident? No...there is no such thing as an accident. Was it Bill? Wait! He didn't do it, but I bet my wanting him to know that nothing was wrong and that I was okay...it was my wanting to comfort him and calm him down. And, it was also him reaching out to me, but not consciously trying so hard. It was both of us trying to accomplish the same thing, but putting the concern for the other person first and it was done through love. I think I get it now, but how do I duplicate it?"

Lost in her thoughts, she did not notice and Bill was no longer in the room and the lights were out. She checked the kitchen and finding it empty, checked the grandfather clock in the hall for the time.

"That can't be! But then it always was losing and gaining time. Maybe Bill hasn't been looking after the old clock as much as he used to," she said and drifted up the stairs to the bedroom. There she found Bill sound asleep with Tippy leaned up against him at the foot of the bed.

"Boy, how did he get up here and asleep so fast?" Christina went around to Bill's side of their bed to his alarm clock. It read 12:00 midnight, just a minute faster than the grandfather clock. "My gosh, it has been two hours since our little episode in the living room. "How could that be? Wait just a second here. I remember all that talk about there not really being any such thing as time. That it was purely a physical measure, but it reality it did not exist. Kind of heavy, I always thought. But thinking back over the date on the calendar, his time certainly did not match my present existence and now it has happened again. But instead of years this time, it was hours. Hey guys...great lesson!" She said to no one in particular, but to anyone who was listening.

"Not bad, huh?"

Christina instantly recognized that beautiful voice and turning around saw the golden ball high in the corner of the bedroom. As if liquid gold, it took the form of Josef.

"I knew if I let you go, you would figure it out by yourself. You have proven yourself to be such a good student already. You are definitely right about the time thing being strictly an Earthly measure. In reality there is no such thing and all things happen simultaneously. You will see this in its full perspective some 'time.' Did you want to go back now or do you want to stay?"

"I would like to stay, but this entire evening has been a bit difficult for me. I think I will come back again and try to duplicate what I did, but for longer."

"I don't want to disappoint you, but it may not happen again. You were partially right in your explanation of how it happened. All the circumstances were just right for it. I am not saying it won't happen again, but I don't want you to be disappointed if it does not. It is not one-sided, but a definite two-way communication with both parties taking full part, be it consciously or unconsciously. There are many things that must occur, besides just the desire. Even the Earth's atmospheric condition can make a difference. It is something similar to a telephone and then being on the best wavelength without any atmospheric interference. The person you are trying to call must be home, or you don't want to get a busy signal, and you don't want to get a hangup (which is kind of what happened to you). It is also helpful if the person you are trying to reach is receptive to the principles, however, not necessary. Perhaps at one time they already had this ability and no longer need it or desire it. Or maybe they want to, but that tiny glimmer of fear of the unknown creeps in and takes over their willingness. All kinds of things come into play here. Actually, anyone can do it if they work at it and desire it and overcome any fears. That is putting it in very simple terms, but you get the idea."

With that he wrapped his huge wings around Christina and before she could even think a goodbye to Bill, they were back in front of her cottage. She actually felt good to be back, instantly feeling lighter. She turned to thank Josef and saw his golden globe blink at her and disappear. Feeling as though she needed to refresh herself from her ordeal, she entered her cottage and visualized a fresh apple and a cup of tea. She knew this wasn't really necessary, but she still felt the need for some "comfort food." While sipping her tea she reflected on the previous events, wondering what happened, and if she would ever get through to Bill. Maybe I can get through to the girls! She felt better already realizing she had not encountered a dead-end to her efforts. She stretched her legs out on her overstuffed couch and rested her head on the arm and stared at the ceiling for a while, before finishing her apple and tea. Of course, the tea never got cold and the apple did not turn brown where she had already taken a bite. "No such thing as time," she thought to herself.

CHAPTER 20

When Christina felt properly renewed, she thought of Felicia and Sarah and they instantly appeared at her door.

"I understand you had a time of it," Felicia said.

"Oh, did I! I became so frustrated with myself and my inability to get through."

"Think about what you just said," suggested Sarah.

"No! Is that what I did? My frustration got in the way? Tell me, is that what happened?"

"Wel-l-l-l, that was only part of it, but a big part of it," Sarah answered. "You know about all the others factors that come into play before you realize success, but I must say it does help if you can stay calm and refrain from the negative feelings you were experiencing."

"Oh, thanks. I needed that boost from someone and it gives me a starting point for the next attempt. Thank you, thank you!"

"One thing I found helped me," Felicia added, "was to remember that life and the afterlife are filled with miracles. Miracles of all kinds. Small ones and big ones. Being able to connect with someone in another realm altogether, is a miracle on both sides. It helps to expect one."

"Oh, I was expecting all right. I just got caught up in expecting and forgot what I was supposed to be doing! I suppose I thought it was all going to happen automatically, just because I wanted it."

Chuckling Sarah responded, "That's perfectly okay. You need to practice a little more balance between expecting and doing, that's all."

"Who's for another trip?" Felicia asked.

"I guess I am...but as I used to say, I need to work up a little dread to face it," Christina answered with some hesitation.

CHAPTER 21

Both girls laughed at her and Felicia grabbed Christina's hand and pretended to be pulling at an immovable object. "You are so kind-hearted, that you have to be reminded that everyone is where they want to be. The people you will see have chosen to suffer, probably because they believe they deserve to suffer. They are creating their own 'hell,' and have all kinds of help to release themselves from their bondage. Granted no deed goes unrewarded or unpunished. It is not all self-inflicted, but they still have help available to right their wrongs and move on to bigger and better things. As they did in life, they are turning their backs on their own spiritual reality," Sarah said with that beautiful twinkle in her eyes and a look of "come on, you can do it!"

Christina smiled back, shrugged and agreed with still a hint of reluctance.

Felicia and Sarah each took one of Christina's hands, all three closed their eyes and they 'landed' in the most dismal place Christina had ever seen. The people were walking around slowly, round-shouldered, looking at the ground, as if they were saying, "There is no light at the end of the tunnel, no hope, nothing can change this."

Christina felt herself being pulled down with them, wanting to go commiserate with them. She was feeling their guilt and their pain and their self-pity. She became cold and was overcome with a feeling of depression. For the first time since arriving here, she was terribly frightened. She looked at Sarah and Felicia and they seemed so far away from her. Mentally she tried to call them, but they didn't seem to hear her. "I don't want to get stuck in this place! What if I can't get out, or get back?" She felt herself being pulled farther down and was beginning to lose sight of the girls. "What is happening? How is this happening?" Christina shouted in a state of panic.

Fortunately, Felicia saw what was occurring instantly, and put her arms around Christina. She and Sarah visualized the white light surrounding and protecting the three of them, also providing the warmth, so obviously missing in this place.

Christina felt as though she was being transported through space and realized she was being embraced by Felicia and Sarah and felt safe and secure again.

Gratefully, Christina said "Thanks. I got caught up, didn't I? I didn't think to surround myself again and was beginning to feel distanced from you. I was so scared I wouldn't be able to leave this place. That I was trapped and I would never get back!"

"It was your fear that trapped you," offered Sarah. "All you had to do was release the fear and reach for the light. But this was a good lesson learned I bet you won't soon forget!"

"Count on it!" Christina said with a tremendous sigh of relief.

"You would not be allowed to stay here, because this is not where you belong. You may choose to come here to help, but you would not be forced to remain and live here. But obviously you did not know that, or hadn't figured it out yet. In time I am sure it would have come to you," explained Felicia. "Now let's try to talk with some of these people, if they feel like it. Most of the time they do, because they are so wrapped up in themselves."

The homes, if you want to call them that, were of the type you would see on Earth in the ghettos, or the wooden shacks of the poor sections of small towns, or tent cities of the middle-east and Africa. Many of these people lived this way while on Earth; however, others had been very well-to-do, living in opulence. Their Earthly life style had nothing to do with their being here.

Although the three girls were walking through a populated area holding hands, dressed in light colors as opposed to the dark grays and browns of the inhabitants, no one looked at, much less spoke to them. Leading the way, Felicia said, "Let's go over and talk to that man sitting in front of his one-room house." As she approached him with Christina and Sarah following about four steps behind, he glanced at them and immediately found something in the dirt by his feet that demanded close attention. Undaunted, Felicia approached him. "Hi! How are you?"

"What do you care? You don't even know me!"

"That doesn't mean I don't care. I am genuinely interested in how you are doing. That is why I walked over here to see you."

"Yeah sure, you and your two nosey friends. You're here to feel sorry for me. Well don't! You and your fancy togs. Comin' in here thinkin' you are better'n me. Well you're not! I don't need you pokin' around here. It was the same way back there. I didn't need them and I don't need you. Now go away and leave me alone! People! Always lookin' for somethin' for nothin'. Nosey, meddlin' folks with nothin' better to do with their time. Go away! Go away! Get outta here!"

"I am sorry to have bothered you, Mr...."

"Mister Nobody, that's who! Get lost."

"Sorry, Mr. Nobody. Maybe I'll see you again sometime."

"Hmpff," he replied as he went back to studying that very interesting spot at his feet.

As they walked away from Mr. Nobody, Felicia turned and looked at the girls and said, "Not a real outgoing sort of fella. It would be a help to him if we silently sent him love. He doesn't have to know we are doing it, for him to feel it."

As the three girls visualized him surrounded in love, he glanced up at them as they walked away before returning his gaze to his interesting spot in the dirt.

The three moved toward a plump woman in her late 50's or so, as she swept the stoop of her very small shack. Her eyes looked as though they were capable of housing a twinkle; instead they were harboring a dull look of bitterness. This time Sarah approached her saying "Good day, Mrs. Vanderholt. How are you doing?"

Mrs. Vanderholt uttered her response in an exhausted sigh. "Okay, I guess. Nothing I do around here is appreciated."

"Oh? What have you been doing?" Sarah asked.

"Well, look at me now, I am sweeping trying to make this place look better, and do you think anyone notices? No. Do you think anyone else would do the same to make his or her place look better? No. Look at those places. They are filthy dumps."

"But your place looks nice and clean Mrs. Vanderholt. That should please you."

"Not much, when you look around you. I don't want to live in a dump like this. I go over to those people and tell them to clean up their mess. It looks like crap. But do they listen to me? Of course not! I have even resorted to screaming at them that if they want to better themselves they need to live better. Fix their places up. Show up the other people on this street. What is everyone going to think of them, living like this? Not that I care mind you, but I don't want them as neighbors if they can't keep up. And I sure don't want anyone saying I am a slob, when I am not. I have always only wanted the best for myself. Is that so wrong? I had the money, so why not spend it the way I wanted. It was 'my' money, after all."

"You are right that you had a lot of money. Remember that little girl at your church that needed surgery and didn't have the insurance to cover it? Your money could have helped that little girl."

"Maybe. But that wasn't my fault - it was her parents. Maybe if he had worked a little harder and not lost his job, they would have had the money for her surgery. Her surgery was not my responsibility. It was her parents. He was nothing but a bum anyway. Did you see how they lived? I couldn't be expected to take care of everyone with a problem. I would have been broke in no time. Anyway, enough people chipped in and the little girl had her surgery. So it all worked out okay without my help. I don't know why everyone expects the person with the money to come to the rescue of anyone with a problem. It doesn't work that way. If they were supposed to have the money, they would have had it. Obviously, they were meant to be poor. I was meant to be rich. We get what we deserve."

"It is true that you were rich in life. What are you here? I don't think it was about money at all, but love. Whatever you give in love, returns to you tenfold."

"Nonsense! It will get better here. You'll see. I will change these people in time. They will come around to my way of thinking. I'll make this place a showplace. You'll see. Come back and see me later, if you don't believe me. It'll be a showplace. Yep, a real showplace, without the riffraff," Mrs. Vanderholt said as her voice became more and more of a whisper as if disappearing in thought. She resumed sweeping her stoop and the girls could hear her still talking in that exhausted tone as they walked away.

"More?" Sarah asked.

"It's okay. I am seeing what you mean by being wrapped up in themselves. Is there someone like Angela here to help them too?" asked a concerned Christina.

"Yes, of course. No matter where we are, here or on Earth, there is always help available, if we just seek it, and open our minds to it. These people are definitely not alone, however, some prefer to think they are, refusing to seek help on any level," Sarah answered.

"Don't the ones that are here to help, offer that help to the ones that really need it?"

"No. They all really need it. The help would be rejected, believing themselves to already be nearly perfect. It would be considered meddling in things that don't concern them. They never did anything wrong. To ask for help you have to recognize that you need it, or perhaps did something wrong," explained Sarah.

"Then how do they explain their being here in this awful place?" asked Christina.

"As in everything else in their lives, it is someone else's fault. It is certainly not through their doing. They shouldn't be here. It is all a big mistake. One day it will be straightened out and then everyone will know they were right all along. And someone will apologize to them for the crime committed against them," Sarah continued. "I have heard it over and over again and it is nearly always the same with only slight variations. They had the problem in life of accepting the responsibility of their own actions and that did not change simply because they 'died.' It is always so much easier to blame someone else."

Christina nodded, saying, "I have known people like that. Even people that I have loved and been close to. It must be painful for them and take a lot of joy out of their lives, believing there is always someone out to get them."

"Precisely why they are here. Some of life's lessons are difficult and if not learned during life on Earth, they are ultimately learned regardless of where we are," interjected Felicia, who had been silent since they had left Mr. Nobody.

"Something is bothering you Felicia. What is it?" asked Christina. "You have been so quiet and I must say I don't know of anyone who would consider you necessarily quiet."

Quickly jerking her head toward Christina as though she had just been aroused from a deep sleep, Felicia hesitated and answered, "I was visiting some old memories, that's all. I am not as much bothered as I am looking back. One of my recent lives on Earth was not what some people would call easy. And that is not a problem either. My Father walked out on my Mother and me when I was only 8 years old. It was a blow to me and even harder on my Mother. I was certain I must have done something wrong to make him leave. The guilt set in and I became somewhat unruly.

"Mother was unable to keep a job for longer than a month at a time. She became unpredictable, had sudden temper tantrums, and cried a lot. Her health seemed to be suffering. My Grandparents stepped in and sought help for my Mother and took me to live with them. In spite of the help, my Mother had a mental breakdown. She was institutionalized and I didn't see her again until I was old enough to understand...almost 13 years old. Mother was living in her own private world of her own making. When she saw me she smiled at me, but it was an empty smile with no facsimile of recognition.

"Fortunately, I had the love of my Grandparents, but I still missed the love of my Mother and Father. As wonderful as my Grandparents were, it was not the same as being with your parents. However, my Grandparents were patient with me, tolerant of my irritability, and provided a close and warm environment for me.

"I never knew what happened to my Father, until the first time I arrived here. When I saw Mr. Nobody, I immediately recognized him. He was my Father. I wanted to go to him and put my arms around him and tell him it was all right. I wanted to feel him touch me. But he does not recognize me at all because of his continued self-absorption. I continue to send him light for his awakening and I continue to wait.

Each time I come here and see him I hope he will recognize me and know the love I always had for him.

"There are still things we have to contend with while over here. I am still learning and I know he is too, even if a bit slowly. He has a lot more to overcome than I did.

"Thanks for your concern, but I am fine. There is so much for him to do and I want to be there for him."

Christina shook her head as if lost in thought herself and said, "How do you separate yourself from the situation? Isn't it hard? Isn't he still your Father? Doesn't it hurt?"

"Hey, hey. One question at a time please, little Miss Impatient," Felicia said grinning at her inquisitive friend. "At first I was very involved with his dilemma and it was hard for me. And yes, he was my Father and although we are still connected, he is no longer my Father. Yes, it did hurt at first, but I have reached an understanding now. But as we used to say on Earth, 'It only hurts for a little while.' We will be together again and again, but in many different relationships.

"For now, I will wait and will be there for him when he asks. Then I will do whatever I can to help. Right now he is on his own, because he wants it that way. We have each chosen our own way and it is not up to anyone else to interfere. We must be invited to help."

A look of puzzlement crossed Christina's face and looking first to Sarah and then to Felicia, asked, "Is that why you two are with me? Did I invite you to help me?"
In unison, both girls responded with laughter, "NO!"

Sarah hugged Christina and said, "Your situation is different because you have not put yourself into a state of self-punishment and denial. We were sent to you as friends and temporary teachers. To show you the 'sights,' so to speak... your personal tour guides. We have always been friends and will always be friends. Remember, we have been together before and will be again. This is our pleasure."

"Thanks," Christina said with a sigh of relief. "Don't get me wrong. I wouldn't mind if you had been sent to me, it was just that I was afraid I might have been avoiding something important and was going to need a slap on the wrist or something."

"If that were the case, we would have slapped your wrist long ago! No point in putting off the inevitable!"

All three giggled at that like a bunch of schoolgirls. Christina's giggle was more in the form of relief than in a funny 'ha-ha' sort of way. Schoolgirl was just the way Christina felt at this moment

CHAPTER 22

Christina's thoughts carried her away to the park behind her childhood home and the woods with the creek she spent hours exploring. She was so lost in her own thoughts that she hardly noticed the subtle changes taking place. Both Sarah and Felicia knew what was happening, but chose to remain silent and follow along. Still in her reverie, Christina was listening to the birds and the smell of the damp richness of decaying leaves and mosses all filling her senses. She believed herself to be traveling down memory's path, but when a sound startled her she came to. She looked around and found herself standing in the middle of the old and familiar woods with the small creek lazily wandering through her beloved trees at the bottom of a small ravine. Startled, she looked around for Sarah and Felicia, who were amusedly standing behind her watching and enjoying Christina's creation.

Christina sheepishly grinned and said, "Guess I felt I needed a break, huh?"

"It's okay. We all do that from time to time. Back on Earth we would have called it spacing out! And in a way, I suppose we are," Felicia countered. "Anyway -- show us around. It must have been a special place for you."

"I suppose you would call it special. I sure spent a lot of hours here with my best friend. We loved exploring the woods, hunting for unusual stones, making walking canes out of fallen branches, crossing the creek using nature's stepping stones. In the name of progress, the city was installing man-sized pipes to divert the creek. However, to us it was a natural "horse cave," where our voices would echo and we made sounds like horse's hooves. It became our special hideout. No one could find us there (or so we thought). There are so many fond and warm memories. Come on! I'll show you."

Christina took off running down the medium grade to the creek. Exactly like when she was a child, she jumped cautiously from rock to rock enabling her to cross the small stream. Both Felicia and Sarah followed her every step, rock by rock, enjoying their adventure enormously. On the other side of the creek Christina ran along side it following its bends and curves leading to the oversized drainage pipe. Once there she entered the pipe and shouted as she did as a child, listening to the echoes bounce around the inside. Felicia and Sarah playfully joined in shouting and singing. Laughing, all three girls plopped down on the floor of the pipe, out of breath and somewhat damp, but happy. The pipe had not been installed yet and was just sitting in place, allowing some of the creek water to enter, but not completely flow through. Playing follow-the-leader, Christina led the girls stomping through the puddles of still water, obviously put there for their own amusement and fun. Christina spread out her arms as if to fly, pretending to be a hawk and the others followed. Imagine Christina's surprise, suffering a momentary lapse of memory as to where she really was, when she lifted off the ground with arms outstretched and soared over the pipe, the creek, and the woods. Reveling in this wonderful, new ability, she literally tried out her wings. She flew over her childhood home, her neighborhood, her park. She checked out her schoolyard. She was the hawk. Soaring back to the park, with her extra keen eyes she saw the chipmunks scampering across the ground hiding in hollowed logs, the squirrels playing tag in the trees, even butterflies, flitting from flower to flower. She looked over her shoulder and saw her companions right behind her, as if still playing follow-the-leader. In the air, all three did loop-the-loops, dived, soared and enjoyed the freedom of the sky they all had dreamed of as physical children. Eventually, they landed back in their large pipe and all three sat silently, smiling at each other, no words necessary.

Reluctantly, Christina said, "I guess we should get back to where we were, huh?"

"No problem. This was so enjoyable, and since time is not an issue, it was a welcomed break for us all. We don't have to be anywhere," offered Sarah.

CHAPTER 23

For a while the girls continued to sit in silence, listening to the sounds of the woods and the gentle current of the creek falling over Christina's stepping-stones. None of the three were terribly anxious to leave.

Feeling refreshed, as though they had been on a vacation that Christina's daydream of reminisces created for them, they returned.

Looking around her at the self-absorbed people inhabiting this place, and the negative energies they were creating for themselves, Christina understood why she took leave.

"This could really be depressing if I allowed myself to be influenced by it," she thought to herself.

"Remember asking if there was an 'Angela' here to help these people?" Felicia asked.

"Yes, of course. I realize now, there must be."

"The 'Angela' here is called Hath," Felicia began.

"And this is someone we really want you to meet," Sarah chimed in.

"Lead the way!" suggested Christina.

Once more playing follow-the-leader, Felicia pretended walking a tightrope, arms out for balance, and the others imitated her, looking very out of place in their dismal surroundings. All still feeling a little high from their short vacation.

Felicia stopped in front of a shanty of the same disrepair, but different in that there was a single daffodil in a pot on the windowsill. An unusual sight, it looked very out of place among the drab colors, lent a hint of hope. She stepped up to the door and knocked The door swung open as if ordered to do so. A gentleman, looking as though born into the aristocracy, but dressed in wrinkled, soiled coveralls and needing a shave, warmly greeted them.

"Felicia! And whom hath you brought with you?"

"Hi, Hath! Good to see you again. I'd like you to meet Christina, and of course you remember Sarah."

"Why, of course I do! How could anyone forget lovely Sarah?" With that Hath bowed and took Sarah's hand. "And Christina, you are another beauty just as the two who are with you. I am truly blessed this day!" Turning to Sarah he asked, "What hath brought you here?"

"We are taking Christina on a tour and we are her travel guides," she answered with a teasing tone in her voice.

"It would seem to me there would be a lot more pleasurable places in which to entertain your new friend," he responded. "With such beauty as hers you should be taking her to the Castle of the Angels not cavorting down here with the likes of me and my friends!"

Obviously, Christina thought, this was a game they all took pleasure in playing with each other. It was all done with such good nature.

Turning to Christina Hath said, "You hath chosen your friends well, my dear. I am sure they will show you a good time...once you leave here." He turned to Felicia, winked and smiled broadly.

Christina liked Hath immensely. It was though she had known him forever, although he certainly didn't look like anyone she had ever known.

With that, he turned toward her and smiled then seemed to turn liquid, shimmering and swirling like oil moving on water. When the movement stopped, he was standing before her in an elegant white suit, with vest of course, ruffled shirt with wide cuffs and white shoes. A white cane and top hat would have rounded out the picture. In a state of shock, Christina decided there were no words to aptly describe Hath's appearance. No matter what word she selected -- classy, sensational, aesthetic, magnificent, majestic -- it fell short.

Bowing to Christina, Hath said, "Thank you my dear, you are too kind."

Stunned, Christina thought to herself, "Darn! I did it again! I left myself wide open for that one! I must learn to check my thoughts sometime." She gave an embarrassed smile to Hath, who returned a knowing one.

"I am here with my friends, by choice. I could see the question in your eyes. What in the world is he doing here? I come and go, but am here at the disposal of anyone that needs to talk, needs help, or just a break from their self-inflicted monotony.

"These people are here, because this is what they expected. Which is basically true of all the levels here. Their personal belief was that they were never dealt the hand they deserved in life, so why should it be any different here. Some believe they are in purgatory, awaiting something better. Some believe this is all there is. Others are finally coming around to the understanding that the change must come from within themselves. One of the common held beliefs in life is that once you 'die' you will wear white gowns and will know everything there is to know and will sit at the right hand of God. To me that would seem somewhat boring. How about you?"

A little dumbstruck to hear talk like this here, Christina slowly nodded to her host.

"You simply pick up where you left off. It is as simple as that. Your belief systems don't change because you 'died.' Learning never ends until we reach the stage of perfection and become integrated with the Universal Mind, or God Consciousness and return to our beginning. You have heard the expression 'we are all God in the making.' God is expressing Himself as you. It is our job to learn, love, experience, feel, give, receive, and live life to its very fullest, as our gift to God. Man is not perfect and is not expected to be perfect. There are no expectations, man simply is. He has many, many chances to become perfect, and he will return to do it over and over again until he gets it right. It's just that each time it will become less difficult. It is man's responsibility to do his very best for himself and then for others; so you see, nothing changes here. These people are where they choose to be and it is not wrong for them to choose this. They are in a learning process, as we all are. No one is more or less than anyone else, you ARE. These people here are working on it, and that is why I am here also – to help them.

"Let me show you something. Would you like to go on a little trip with me?"

With smiling faces and nodding heads as children waiting to go to Disneyland, the three girls anxiously agreed to the trip.

Indicating they should all hold hands, Hath grew and enfolded them with powerful wings until they all appeared as a missile-shaped white light, and they sped away. In what could be called a second, time-wise, they all landed softly on gentle sloping hills resembling meadows, soft green velvet with clumps of trees in small groves.

To the right, in the distance, Christina saw an area that was fenced off with a very tall wooded fence. For some reason, this seemed very strange to her. "Maybe it is for animals or something," Christina thought. As she turned to her left, down in a very small valley composed of two rolling hills moving off in different directions, sat another area fenced off. Turning to her left again, on top of a distant hill among clumps of tall shade trees, barely visible was the outline of yet another fence.

Seeing the quizzical look appear on Christina's and her traveling friends' faces, Hath nodded toward the nearest fenced area. "You are wondering what that is," he guessed with a hint of a smile on his glowing face. "That, my dears, is a group of people who belonged to an organized religion, that claim to be the only one holding the truth of the real God and His teachings. They are in their 'heaven' of their own making according to their still-held beliefs. In this they are limiting themselves, and confining themselves to this one area and in a kind of limbo with no stretches, learning, growing for the time being. Only when they realize all religions held the truth, and that everyone and everything is a part of the Whole, or All That Is, will they be released from their own incarceration."

"What is it like in there?" asked Christina.

"Let's hold hands one more time and we will enter unseen behind my wings."

Once again they held hands and were lifted up and over the fence. Much to Christina's surprise, it was beautiful inside. The sidewalks were of gold, everyone was walking around in white robes, and there were flowers of every color, trees of every shape and size and birds singing. Hearing music, Christina and the girls turned toward the music and saw a huge cathedral, also in gold. Walking toward the cathedral and approaching the huge doors, they paused on the threshold and peered inside. It was more magnificent that any of the girls had ever seen on Earth, with stained glass windows depicting numerous scenes from the Bible, pearl inlaid pews, velvet cushioned seats, statues of the Virgin Mary and Jesus, with winged angels all along the side walls under the windows facing the pews. There was a man playing and enormous pipe organ with four keyboards, the sounds emitted nearly shaking the walls. There were people throughout the cathedral either with bowed heads in prayer or speaking in hushed whispers to one another, each carrying their Bible or reading passages from it.

As Christina, Felicia and Sarah looked in, a gentleman in a white and gray robe entered the podium area. Waiting for the organ music to stop he stood smiling at the people congregated in front of him. Silence. He raised both hands toward the people in front of him and blessed each one for having been saved by Jesus while in their Earthly form and here and now was their eternal reward. "You are in heaven, soon to be seated at the right hand of God. You must be patient, and ask for forgiveness of all your sins while you were in your Earthly bodies. Your prayers and adoration must not stop now, just because you are in heaven. You will earn the privilege to sit at God's right hand. Your day is coming. Praise God!"

Startled, Christina asked, "Why don't they just walk outside the fence and see what is out there?"

"Because, my dear, they don't know there is anything out there. They believe it is all right here, where they are. They are bringing their belief systems from Earth to this place and creating it here. On Earth, as it is in heaven. They must learn to go beyond their immediate surrounding and belief systems, which will take time. They are here because they want to be. We are all so much more than we believe ourselves to be. It takes time to learn that. Each one of the fenced areas is a different group of religious beliefs. Each one believing they are the only ones who have earned the right of admittance into heaven."

"What about the people who believe in hell? Where are they? What has happened to them?" Christina asked anxiously.

"It is not something you should dwell on, my dear. However, we create with our beliefs. It is not as torturous as the religious leaders would have had us believe, because a loving God would not permit that to happen to his children. But it definitely is a learning experience and there is help with them at all times, guiding and directing them to look beyond themselves. You will have a glimpse of it on your journeys, but I doubt that you will remain there long. Please remember, that man brings this on himself, by himself, by his own choice. Just as easy is his ability to change it, because each and every one of us is greater than what he sees or even knows. It is the hangover of the physical personality we are struggling to overcome, and once this is done we are able to break free of the bondage we have placed ourselves in. Then the true memory sets back in. It is all temporary. Even this place is temporary for the people residing here. The area itself will be here until mankind realizes there is truth in everything and we are all the same part of the whole. Inseparable, undivided, and however unique, ONE. Man will one day become open-minded rather than narrow-minded."

Felicia said, "Even though this place is beautiful, I find it rather depressing and I would like to leave here."

"Me too," chimed in the other two girls.

With that, they felt the security of Hath's wings wrapped around them, then the whooshing sound and the gentle landing in front of Hath's house.

"This place feels better than the one we left!" exclaimed a surprised Sarah.

"We had never seen that place before, although we have been here for a while and were selected to be Christina's guide," said Felicia. "It never stops, does it?" she asked Hath.

"Learning? It never stops, no matter where or who we are. It is our learning and our experiences that are our gifts to God. We are God expressing Himself. He experiences through us. We are His vehicle. Perhaps in this way you can see that there is no right and no wrong, there only IS. We are in the process of becoming. In this regard it is our responsibility, with the knowledge we obtain, to be the very best that we can be.

"Once this is achieved as individuals, then it can be achieved by mankind as a whole. So you see, there is no lazy man's way out. We are not only working to achieve perfection as individuals, but we are doing it for mankind. For one another. For brotherhood. For US."

Hath's musical voice was compelling and Christina, as well as Felicia and Sarah, found themselves hanging on his every word. At the same time they could feel the love emanating from him and surrounding each of them.

"I believe we hath spent enough time together for this session, however I would deem it a pleasurable gift if you would but bless me with another visit soon," Hath said slipping back into his facade of the earlier part of the visit.

"I have to go," Christina announced.

"We will be going back as soon as we make one more stop," offered Felicia.

"No, I have to go now!" Christina exclaimed. And as if it were a magic act - poof! - Christina disappeared.

Felicia and Sarah dumbfounded, looked at each other and then at Hath for an explanation.

Hath replied, "She hath gone where she is needed."

CHAPTER 24

Christina was pulled to her daughter Karen's bedside. Her husband Scott, was clearly in an agitated state and sat by her bed, puffy-eyed holding her hand. His sandy-colored hair hung down his forehead, stubble covered his chin, and his clothes looked as though they had been slept in and probably had. He would sit next to Karen, then jump up and pace the floor before returning to her limp hand once again. He would mumble to himself then aloud, beseech Karen to open her eyes, or at least show some signs of knowing he was there. Christina saw he was obviously in a state of panic.

Karen and Scott had been to South America on a business trip for Scott. They took several extra days for sight seeing and touring before returning home. Karen had become ill with an upset stomach and slight fever the day before their return flight home. By the time they had reached home her fever had elevated to a dangerous point and she had to be removed from the plane by stretcher. The fever stubbornly refused to break. Dr. Hamilton, whom the airline had called in, escorted Scott and Karen to their home rather than a hospital, at Scott's insistence. Also allowing it could be a contagious disease was a deciding factor. At a loss, Dr. Hamilton consulted several other doctors on the staff at his hospital trying to determine from what the fever had originated. At one point they thought she had contracted malaria, at another it was food poisoning, and it was finally decided it must have been from some kind of insect bite. Anti-venom was out of the question, since they had no idea what the possible insect had been, and they were at a loss for any kind of treatment, other than wait it out and hope for the best, watching her closely.

Karen, in her feverish delirium was calling, "Mommy? Mommy?" This summons being the impetus that propelled Christina to her side.

As a Mother for her child, Christina was feeling a deep concern, worry and anxiety for the helpless body lying before her.

Even in her worried haze, she noticed not only Scott at her side, but also two magnificent Beings of a golden-white light standing on either side of her. Just seeing them there gave Christina a sense of well being and the knowledge that it would be all right.

As she bent over to kiss her daughter's forehead, she watched Karen sit up away from her body and rise toward her. Smiling she reached out for her Mother's hand and said, "I am coming with you."

A white light surrounded Christina and her daughter that formed a kind of tunnel, which Christina knew had been created by the Beings of Light. Upon seeing the smiling face of her youngest, Christina thought to herself how beautiful her little girl was. Only now she was virtually glowing. Her short blonde hair framing that beautiful, pixie face with her large blue eyes and a mouth that appeared to be in the beginnings of a perpetual smile, made Christina ache to be with her and touch her. She reached out to her and as they touched, you could not tell where one ended and the other began. All boundaries disappeared.

At first, not knowing where the words were coming from, then realizing she was receiving them from the Beings with her daughter, she answered, "No, my darling, you cannot. That time will come, but it is not now. You have important things to do here yet. Things that you ordained before you came here. You and Scott will be parents soon and your child is waiting for your readiness. There is much joy ahead. Now you must fight. I promise you we will be together again. I will always be here for you when you need me, and even when you don't. Just know that I love you."

"But I want to come with you. It feels so wonderful to be free of the aches and pains of the body. I feel free and alive."

"I know. But you will remember this always, and when the real time comes you will know there is nothing to fear, and instead will rejoice in it. And I will be waiting here for you. But not now. Go back and be happy."

Reluctantly, Karen turned and floated back to the body lying on the bed. She turned back and looked at her Mother and mouthed the words, "I love you, Mommy."

Christina mouthed the words back, "I love you too, honey."

As she returned to the feverish body, Scott saw her eyes flutter and heard her whisper, "I love you, Mommy," as a smile appeared on her face.

The two Beings bent over her and covered her in their golden-green light.

Christina knew her daughter was in the best hands possible. Before going back she wanted to check on Anne. The mere thought transported her to the den of Anne's home, where Anne was sprawled out on the couch reading and John was working on his computer. It was quiet as they were both doing what they loved, and together.

It gave Christina a warm feeling all over to see her other beautiful daughter looking so happy and contented. She knew Anne had a good marriage and had a full, enriched life ahead of her. Anne was beautiful in an altogether different way from Karen. With her long, dark blonde hair, crystal blue eyes that reflected the sadness of an imperfect world, she had a statuesque beauty about her, as though she should be set in porcelain and placed on a shelf for all to see. There was a vulnerability about her that always touched Christina's heart. Reaching out to her mentally, Christina sent a wave of energy to her oldest daughter.

"John?"

"Hmmm?"

"Did you just notice anything?"

"Like what?"

"I don't know…a change. Maybe a little bit cooler, or a breeze or something."

"No, but my computer screen shuddered a little, like there had been a power surge. Why?"

"I don't know…maybe it was nothing."

Christina sent another burst of energy.

"There! Do you smell anything?"

"Uhm…yeah. Is that a new perfume you are wearing?"

"No, silly. I'm not wearing any. What you are smelling is Mom's perfume!"

"Yeah, right."

"Well, it is!" Anne replied as she looked back to her book, but didn't read.

Christina said, "I love you Anne."

Anne looked up quickly, "Okay, now! Did you hear that?"

"What?"

"Did you hear anything that sounded like tiny bells? And feel warm all over?"

"Just a minute ago you said cool and a breeze…now you are warm. But I'll admit to another power surge on the computer screen. Are you all right?"

"Of course I am. But I have to call Karen. Now."

"Don't you think it's a little bit late for that? They just got back today from their trip and they have probably gone to bed early to catch up on their jet lag. Why don't you wait until morning?"

"No! I have to call now!"

After hanging up from talking to Scott, Anne turned to John and with tears running down her cheeks told him about Karen.

"I know that was Mom a few minutes ago, telling me about Karen and prompting me to call. Even your computer knew. I am going up to bed to meditate for a while and to send Karen some healing light. Scott said she has come out of her deliriums and the fever appears to be breaking. But I still want to help all I can from here. I'll go see her in the morning. Good night, John. I love you." Then quietly to herself she whispered, "I love you Mom, and thanks."

"Good night, Anne. I love you, too. I'll be up in a few minutes."

With that, John said to the empty room, "If that really was you Mom, thanks." His computer screen jiggled once again.

CHAPTER 25

Christina returned to Felicia and Sarah, and said goodbye to Hath, as the three headed out for their next adventure.

Christina felt as though she left part of herself with her family, while being here at the same time. She had heard Scott tell the doctor that Bill was on the way over to be with his daughter. Christina missed Bill terribly. Fleetingly she wondered when he would be here with her, wishing it would be soon. Then feeling guilty about maybe willing his life to end on Earth, she mentally canceled the thought.

"You thinking about it won't make it happen, you know," offered Sarah trying to help Christina with her feelings of separation from her family. "He will make that decision, not you. And it is all right to miss him and want him by your side again. You were good together. Know that you will be again."

"I do feel better knowing that he is going to be with Karen and Scott. I was torn between staying and returning here. I always felt that as long as I was there, that everything would be okay," Christina said with a far-away look in her eyes that matched her fading voice. "If it is this hard for me, I cannot imagine what it must be like for him. And the girls! At least I get to see them whenever I want to and they cannot do that. At least not yet. But with their knowledge and background, they should, one day."

"Some people are not meant to accomplish that feat. And try as they might, that ability will not come to them. It is just that their spiritual energies are aimed in another direction that is right for them. That particular ability has nothing to do with the level of spiritual development or knowledge. Perhaps they already had that ability in another lifetime or maybe it is yet to come," explained Felicia.

"Do you feel up to another journey, now?" asked Sarah.

"Sure. I know my loved ones are all in good hands. I saw the Beings of Light with Karen and somehow I know they will be there for the rest of the family through this. I will check back in on them all when this journey is over. Okay?"

"Of course, it's okay. You are free to go back at any time. Or you are free to journey with us. So, if you are ready, let's go," suggested Sarah.

The girls, standing in a circle, put their arms around each other's shoulders forming a dome, surrounded themselves with light and left Hath's domain.

Where they landed this time was a shock to Christina. Suddenly she was not certain she wanted to be here. She felt very cold and remembered to cloak herself in protective warmth. The looked to Felicia and Sarah and realized they were doing the same thing. She heard a sound and it was not the sound of celestial music she heard at her home, but more like crying.

"What is that noise?" she asked.

"That is the cry of the people here. The volume rises and falls as people come and go to and from this place. It is the sound of the residents bemoaning their undeserved plight, their surroundings, and their situations; just knowing they certainly don't belong here! And not knowing or understanding there is a way out. A simple way," said Felicia.

"Why doesn't someone just show them or tell them? This place is awful!"

"Because there are no shortcuts! No one can tell them. They must discover this on their own. Just like everyone else. These people are no different than you and me. They just think they are. These are the people who have never recognized or accepted the Divine spark within themselves; the ones that could never see beyond themselves. The ones full of hate and loathing for their fellow man and who lacked respect for all living things, nature, animals, Mother Earth...and most of all... themselves," Sarah explained.

"Is this hell, then?" asked Christina.

"Perhaps you could call it that; however, it is of their making. There is not a hell, as a place that we heard about growing up. Those who dwell here have created this hell. It has been created through negativity, hate, mistrust, fear, ignorance and misuse of their gift of life on Earth.

"There are no mistakes. There are no accidents. Tragedies, murders, untimely deaths, abuses of every kind, are all part of the great scheme of things for each individual. Some of these people here are the perpetrators of these deeds. They were the vehicles for the experience, both on their part and on the part of the victim. Those that have been able to understand and see the larger picture and have learned to love their victims as well as themselves have gone on. The victims also chose that experience for their life on Earth both for themselves and their victimizer. Another aspect of this is Karma; the 'Law of Cause and Effect.' All actions are rewarded. And the rewards are not necessarily sweet rewards. But they are just. The reward may not come in that lifetime, but may in another. Whatever you do in life returns to you in kind...and sometimes tenfold. Love and only love, can erase Karma. An individual can learn this on Earth, or here. It doesn't matter. It will be learned." Felicia said with a broad sweep of her hand, "We reap what we sow."

It was gray, dark, dismal and cold. Christina wondered how anyone could stand being here any longer than a few moments, let alone a day, a month or eternity, if that is how long it took some people. Then she realized she was thinking in linear time again, and it just took as long as it took. There were no days, months, years. As she turned to take in the entire surroundings, she saw lean-to's, hovels... dark and dreary...everywhere she looked.

"How can they ever learn to love, if this is all they ever see? This is so depressing and a very difficult place in which to love anything!"

Sarah spoke up with her explanation, "They can begin by loving another. The surroundings will not prevent that, no matter how depressing. And, as on all the other levels, they have help here. This is not an eternal place and believe it or not, no one stays here an interminable length of time. Would you?"

Christina laughed and said, "I wouldn't be here as long as I already have, if I could help it."

The three girls drifted down a slight grade toward what appeared to be a hole in a rock wall. As they approached, Christina noticed it was a cave! Within the walls she heard voices and crying and moaning. She bent down to peer inside and saw several people actually living together, whereas in the area they just left, the other few she had seen appeared to be strictly alone.

At the left wall there was a couple who were shouting and yelling at each other, while opposite them was a man actually comforting a crying woman. There were others sitting and staring blankly into the center of their haphazard circle. On the far wall there were two women huddled together for warmth. All were dressed in ragged, dirty, gray clothing. It reminded Christina of the books she had read about the early leper colonies, where people had been banished to islands, caves or remote non-populated areas, often without benefit of anything material except the clothes on their backs.

It occurred to Christina that these people were learning to integrate with others on a social level, even if they were arguing or fighting as the first couple she noticed. To the rear of the cave, back against the wall to the right of the two women providing warmth to each other, Christina noticed a light beginning to form. It grew until it materialized into a recognizable human form. The Being smiled and beamed warmth toward the three girls. Felicia and Sarah, whose attention had been elsewhere, both looked up and waved.

"Hi, Rafina! We were just telling our friend Christina about you...well, sorta!" Sarah burst out, then quickly and demurely looked at her feet with a guileless smile.

"Oh, stop, Sarah! I know what you meant. No need to chastise yourself." Turning to Christina, he said, "Welcome to our humble abode."

Christina smiled at Rafina and thanked him, while inwardly wishing she wasn't in this place. She noticed that not one individual looked up or gave any indication they heard anything.

"It is true, Christina. They do not know any of us are here. This group is just on the verge of developing an awareness of the existence of something other than themselves. They are beginning to extend themselves beyond their egos. I work with them on the mental level, sending them love, guidance and suggestions. It is so subtle, they are unaware of my energy. A little at a time. 'Easy does it' is our motto here.

"Too much at once would actually be overwhelming, and might affect them adversely causing them to turn away from that previously unknown feeling. This level is mostly made up of souls that are new to this side of life. They are carrying with them the scars, hurts and fears of their Earthly life, never believing they deserved more than what they received in their physical existence. For the majority of these dwellers, it does not take long at all to recognize and know their divine nature, at least on some level, which is the first step to release. Love is the avenue of escape from this level. Look around. You can see evidence of that beginning to happen. Even the arguing couple shows signs of caring, or else they would not be interested in making each other understand their point of view. Granted it is not an out and out show of affection as you and I might know it. But it is caring, nonetheless. It is a start - and a grand one, I might add! "A very important point here, is that everyone…absolutely everyone…is deeply loved and cared for by God. No one is forgotten, no one is ignored, no one is written off as 'bad,' no one is beyond hope or help, and no one is condemned to a burning hell for eternity. Love. That is what it is all about. Love. God's love for His children, as we all are; man's love for his children, man's love for his fellow man, nature, animals, planet Earth, and so it goes. Love. It is so simple. Man makes it difficult."

"So is this the place that people would refer to as Hell?" Christina asked.

Rafina looked at Christina with crystal, blue eyes that seemed to hold truths from the beginning of time. As she felt she was about to fall into their depths, he said, "Hell is the absence of harmony. This can be anywhere, anytime. People are in hell over and over again during their lifetimes, and as you can see…after. Once harmony is established in any area of our lives and our 'after-lives,' there is no longer a hell. Seek harmony, welcome harmony, live in harmony. That is, harmony with yourself, with others, within situations, in your homes, in your workplaces, and in Nature . This can be easily done with love. Love yourself, love others, and love your current situation even if you are desirous of change. With love, it can be changed."

Christina was running her fingers through her hair, seemingly absentmindedly, but was remembering the difficult times, even some sad times and visualizing how they could have been changed with harmony. Something as simple as an argument with Bill, which brought stress to them both, could have been avoided or worked out differently.

"Isn't hindsight wonderful?" said Rafina, as he watched Christina ponder with some agony over what was past. "These are truths that take a long time to discover and learn. It is simple to see now, what could have been done differently. However, it was through those disagreements, and disharmony, you learned. It is not all for naught. It would be wonderful to take this knowledge with you going in, and it would save so much time and effort. But that is the point - you need to make the effort. That is called 'growth.' Wouldn't it be wonderful if your entire life was euphonious and required no effort? But what would be learned? Once you know these truths, there is a great amount of effort in putting it into practice. It is all part of the Grand Plan. Practice makes perfect! And it's a long, long process."

Christina smiled at him and his euphemisms, realizing it made such sense even if these catchy phrases were thrown about lightly on Earth.

She found herself longing for the comfort and peace of her cottage. She wanted Bill to be there so she could curl up beside him on the couch and lay her head on his chest and listen to his heartbeat. She wanted to feel his arms around her. Was it wrong to still want these Earthly things, to long for them?

Rafina walked over to her with a knowing look crossing his face like a shadow of a bird's wing, and slipped his arm gently around her shoulder.

"This is all new to you and the separation from your husband seems only moments ago. The love and the desires and yearnings do not just suddenly disappear simply because you have passed over. You and Bill have been together many, many times and will again. This is a strong loving relationship the two of you have built together. It is normal to miss what you have created together. The love will always remain, but the pain of separation, will ease. Before you realize it you will be reunited here on your plane. If the two of you wish to maintain that relationship here, you may do so. Now I believe it is time for you to return to your haven of peace, for it has been a full period of discovery and learning for you. You would do well to rest and ponder what you have seen."

Grateful for his willingness to send her 'home,' Christina looked questioningly at Sarah and Felicia, both of whom looked equally as anxious to return to their own realm. Felicia taking Christina's hand and Sarah following behind, all three paused to nod a loving thank you to Rafina, and they were 'off.'

CHAPTER 26

Soaring through space with no sound or wind, just a sense of movement, they arrived in Christina's front yard. She felt better instantly as the sight and fragrances of her garden blanketed her like a protective, warm cloak. Her mind was still dancing with the experiences acting as the music. Some joyful, some not, but all part of the Universal dance. She bade the girls a farewell with hugs, promising to call after assimilating all that she had seen and heard, and disappeared into her house.

Before she even sat down to rest, she suddenly longed for a sunset. She longed for the feeling associated with a painted sky, the watercolor washing down from pale pink to orange and collecting rich bittersweet at the horizon, the white clouds streaking off into the distance to meet with someone else's horizon, as if for a late appointment.

She stepped outside onto her stoop and miraculously, as ordered, she drank in the most beautiful sunset she had ever witnessed. She let it surround her, embrace her and enfold her...the most real sunset she had ever seen. She could feel it, hear it, taste it, smell it...it was alive! It welcomed her, as she welcomed it. There seemed to be an actual communication.

After losing herself in the beauty, which seemed like forever, she reluctantly retreated to her living room and the couch that blatantly invited her to sit. Giving in, she sat. Resting her head on the high, overstuffed back, she started her reflection of her latest trip. Everything she had seen and heard, she realized she inwardly had always known. This was a refresher course! It was a shocking revelation to her, believing this to be the first time being exposed to any of this. Just as in 'life' she felt a kind of deja-vu. It came to her in a flash and she sat bolt upright!

"I have been here before…I have done this before…I have heard this before…I have seen this before!" Trying to grab hold of the revelation, as if it were a bubble in a glass of water, she felt it burst in her mind's grasp.

Temporarily giving up, she stretched out lengthwise on her couch and very deliberately brought up images of Bill. After all, that is what brought her back here from her last adventure, wasn't it?

She imagined herself curled up with Bill on the couch and her head on his chest, once again. Feeling very natural and easy, she let go of all the emotions of the 'day.' She rested with her head in that very familiar place and listened for the familiar heartbeat. There it was!

Coming out of her reverie, she became sharply aware of Bill's presence. She was sitting next to him on the couch with her head on his chest. However, it was at his (or their) house, not hers! She had transported, once again without even being aware. It happened so fast!

She took this as a sign that she was getting better at this transportation stuff. She could smell his wonderful, familiar body smell, and feel his warm breath on her forehead. Forgetting herself she thought, "I'm back!" That this was a totally irrational thought was not a part of her mindset. She wanted to be back, therefore she would be back. Period.

She looked lovingly up into his face and was startled to realize he was not sharing in the experience. He was looking off into space as if his mind was on vacation. It occurred to her at that instant, that he looked so much older than she remembered. How could this happen? My beautiful Bill? But on closer examination Christina saw that he was still beautiful, only now with roads etched into his forehead from allowing the traffic of woes to transverse it. Thankfully, he looked much more at peace than he had the last time she visited. The lines were not all lines of sorrow, for the wonderful laugh lines were deepened around his mouth and the tiny crow's feet at the corner of each eye had strengthened from his years of smiling. Maybe not still young, but a face full of character, wisdom, life. A new kind of beauty. One that she had expected to see develop over a long period of time together, so as not to be noticed. Also expecting the aging to be done gracefully, together.

She was finding it very difficult to grasp this concept of no time. It seemed as though only days or maybe weeks had gone by, however Bill's appearance belied this. How much time really did pass? She missed the closeness of him, the feel of him, as though it had been years since she left. However, this was not the case as depicted in her mind, recollecting the past events with Sarah and Felicia.

Suddenly struck with the need to see her daughters, Christina reluctantly left the warm, familiar embrace with Bill. She thought to herself, "It felt wonderful, even if it was only one-sided." Stepping away from the couch she tilted her head to one side and smiling, gazed upon that all too familiar face she loved so much, and blowing him a kiss, "Be back," she told him.

She left for Karen's place. She found her at home fixing dinner and humming to herself and obviously back to normal physically, after her ordeal.

"I wonder how much time has passed?" She asked herself. At that moment, Scott walked in the door and admonished his beautiful wife for going all out on an elaborate, candle-light dinner, when she should still be taking it easy.

"Karen, you know the doctor told you to take it easy for a while and not try to rush things."

"I know he did, but I really feel great and wanted to do something special in celebration. It has been too long since I felt this good. I promise, I will take it easy by letting you do the dishes!"

"Oh, thanks!" He walked over and planted a big kiss on her cheek and put his arms around her waist from behind and they stood together rocking slightly for a few moments. "I love you, did you know that?"

Karen turned slightly to look at him without breaking the hold he had on her and grinned and said, "I had a feeling that might be the case, but I wasn't entirely sure. So to make certain you would want to hang around for a while, I fixed this gourmet dinner. Then when you were fat and happy and feeling very cooperative, I planned to lure you to the bedroom. Then I knew I could win you over for sure!"

"You don't need a gourmet dinner to do that. In fact, put that dinner on hold and you can win me over now!"

"Can we go make a baby?"

"Isn't it too soon after your illness?"

"Hey, the doctor said take it easy…he didn't say don't make babies!"

Scott turned her to face him, they kissed and then just stood there holding each other in front of the sink. Neither one wanting to move or to break the spell.

Christina could feel the love surrounding the two and felt a surge of happiness well up in her for her daughter. A baby!

She blew a kiss to her daughter and son-in law and turned to go when it occurred to her at this moment in space that it was not the same time on Earth that she had just left Bill. She was visiting another time! But she didn't feel as though she had crossed any time lines or anything. But what would that feel like anyway? What is happening with Karen now? What is now? When is now? She turned back to look once more at the happy couple and they looked different somehow. They looked a little older, but were still in their embrace in front of the kitchen sink.

Suddenly, she heard, "Mommy! Daddy!" Scurrying into the kitchen was a tiny little toe-headed, two-year-old boy, waving a toy at his Dad, who had just gotten home from work and was giving Mommy the ritualistic "Honey-I'm-home," kiss.

"Fix it, fix it," demanded the toddler.

Swooping the little boy up into his arms, Scott said, "Okay Andy, where is it broken?"

Karen whispered to Scott, "His windup car keeps running down and all day he has been running to me to fix it."

Christina grabbed for her own heart feeling it would burst if she didn't control it. She realized this was just a hang-over from having once owned a body, but the feeling was there. Andrew was her Father's name. And the child! He was so beautiful, a real charmer! She longed to hold him, touch him. She watched the small family for quite some time, and stayed by the child's side through dinner, bath and bedtime. She listened to his bedtime story ready by his Mommy and heard him say his prayers. The same ones she had said with her daughters when they were small.

Scott came into the room and he and Karen kissed the small child "good night," tucked in his side covers, turned out the light and left the room. A small Mickey Mouse night-light glowed on the wall. Christina stood there taking it all in. She moved closer to him at the side of the bed. Tilting her head to one side to angle her face in line with his, she gazed upon that small cherubic face, wanting so much to take him in her arms. Mickey Mouse's glow illuminated her face making her look quite angelic.

"Who're you?" A small voice asked.

Startled at being seen, Christina smiled and said, "Just someone who stopped in to see you and from now on I'll be stopping in a lot."

"'Okay. Cher name?" he asked in his tiny voice.

"Uh, my name is Christina."

"Steena?"

"That's pretty close. In fact, close enough. Why don't you close your eyes now and go to sleep and I will come back and seen you again one day. Okay?"

"Okay. When?"

"Umm, I don't know exactly when...but soon. Okay?"

"Uh huh, sokay." Little Andrew closed his eyes and was instantly asleep.

Feeling giddy inside, Christina left for Anne's.

Anne was at her kitchen table working on a flower arrangement, and John was in their study doing some catch-up work from the office. Anne was humming to herself, completely engrossed in her creative project, and apparently very happy. Just tuning into the vibes in the house, Christina could tell that all was well here.

She walked over to stand behind Anne and admire her work, when Anne stopped what she was doing and turned around and actually faced her Mother. Staring in her direction for a moment, she shrugged and turned back to her flowers. Christina then moved opposite Anne and looked into those blue, blue eyes and sent her love. Anne stopped again, and looked directly at her Mother once more. "Mom? Is that you? Are you here?"

Disappointed that Anne was not really seeing her, Christina said, "Yes, darling daughter, I am here."

Then to Christina's amazement, Anne replied, "I thought so."

"Anne? Can you hear me?"

"Yes, I can hear you! But a little fuzzy. Say something!"

"I want you to know how wonderful it is where I am! I love you so very, very much and miss being able to talk with you and just be with you."

"Okay, Mom. I heard it is wonderful, and you love and miss me, but I lost some of it too. Maybe if we practice this we'll get it down to a fine art. Okay?"

"That would be wonderful"

"I saw your sister and your nephew! He is so beautiful!"

"Andrew? Yes he is adorable. We all just love him. Is this the first you have seen him?"

"Yes, I suppose it is. I have been seeing and learning a lot over there. I have been kept very busy."

"What have you been doing over there? Can you tell me?"

"I can tell you, but it would take a really long time and I don't know if I have the strength to stay in contact that long."

"I'm having some trouble picking you up Mom, but as long as I know you are there and that I can talk to you when I want, then it's okay."

Feeling a bit anxious that their connection would be lost, Christina said quickly and loudly, "Please tell Karen that I was there and that I love her. I love you too, dear one. Give that big husband of yours a kiss for me too, and that little Andrew. Would you?"

"Of course, Mom. Wait! Before you go...John and I are going to have a little girl!"

Christina looked at her daughter and realized she could see a beautiful purple glow coming from her tummy.

"I'll be there for you both and John."

"Come back real soon, please? I have missed you so much. This is wonderful, knowing we can talk like this. I love you too, Mom."

"I love all three of you."

Having accomplished a great feat, Christina felt the need to return home.

Back in her cottage again, Christina sat in her now-familiar, comfy sofa, reflecting on her Earthly experiences and the joy of seeing her grandson. She was extremely grateful to see Karen looking so healthy and Anne so very happy. What more could a Mother ask? Her attention was drawn toward the bookcase housing some of her greatest memories. One in particular was calling to her, where resting between the covers were the warm Mother-memories of reading Winnie-the-Pooh to her girls at bedtime. "I wonder if I could read this book to Andrew? I wonder if I could take it with me on my next visit?" She made the determination to at least try. She also realized there was still a lot she had to learn, and many questions left to ask.

She put these questions at the top of her mental list of things to ask Sarah and Felicia.

CHAPTER 27

Back in Karen's kitchen at breakfast the following morning, she and Scott were having their morning coffee together. Sleepy-eyed and dragging a small blanket behind him, Andrew toddled into the kitchen.

"Good morning, Mr. Sunshine!" Karen greeted her son.

"Mornin' Mommy," he responded.

"Hi, son. Did you have a good sleep?" asked Scott.

"Uh huh. Affer de'lady toll me to."

"Lady? What lady?" asked Karen.

"The perty lady, Mommy. She said she was gonna see me."

"Did this lady tell you who she was?" Karen asked, believing he was dreaming, but hoping otherwise.

"Uh huh. She said she was Steena."

Karen looked at Scott and Scott returned her look of disbelief. They both turned to Andy and in unison asked, "Christina?"

"Uh huh, Steena!"

CHAPTER 28

Needing a bit of rejuvenation, Christina left her cottage to go for a walk as she frequently did when she was "alive." She wanted to touch a tree, hear a bird, smell a flower. At the thought, she was transported to the area of her Magical Forest beside the stream. She drank in the heady aroma of the pine and the delicate scents of the wildflowers as she dipped her hand into the cool stream. The water had a texture unlike anything she had ever experienced before. As it surrounded her fingers, it also began to surround her whole being. The velvety sensation penetrated everywhere. Christina instantly knew she was being cleansed, renewed and revitalized.

Where there had been many thoughts, questions and concerns, there now lived an encompassing peace. She knew she would have the answers to her needful questions. As though it was purposefully placed there, the idea and picture of the schools she had been shown at the beginning of her arrival here came to mind. "I wonder if I could learn to maintain communication with my daughters?" She asked herself. "What about Bill? And my new grandson – how come he can see me? I must go and find out what things are being taught there. And will my granddaughter be able to see me too?"

Desiring the walk, rather than transporting herself, she chose to slowly make her way to the area of the schools, enjoying the flowers, wildlife, fragrances, along the way. Arriving in front of the school where her parents were teaching classes, she waited until class had finished and embraced both parents as they emerged from the classrooms.

In answer to her many questions, her Mother told her, "All manner of things are taught here. In fact, many choose to remain here and learn rather than through the physical experiences on Earth. Of course, it is a different kind of learning and a different path altogether, is followed. Many of the students here choose to work with people in the physical as guides, or to be part of the welcoming committee (so to speak) for new arrivals here, just to mention a couple. There are many different paths to choose from, however, the learning never ceases, no matter where you are. And, yes, you can become adept at communication with Karen, Anne and Bill…and especially that darling, little Andrew and soon-to-be Ashley! Children are more open and receptive, because they have not yet been told there is no such thing as 'ghosts,' or, 'you can't do that!' or, 'you know you are just imagining these things, so stop!' Man does more damage in the name of 'reality' than he realizes. One of the phrases used so often is, 'I am just being realistic!' Just what is 'realistic?' It all goes back to manifesting what you believe. If you believe something to be realistic, then it shall be. So parents can impose their reality on their children, who are in the process of experiencing their own reality, which in many cases is much closer to the truth.

"Anyway, as you can see, I haven't changed much – I am still lecturing and teaching and still tend to go off on tangents, as I did when we were on Earth together!"

Christina's Mother had that twinkle in her eye, just as she used to when telling tales on herself. Christina thought that perhaps some things never changed. It was so good to be with them again, although it was not exactly the same, when it was Mother and daughter, or Father and daughter. The tremendous love was still there, but magnified, and not in an authoritative way as in parent/child. On Earth, the child is always the child no matter what the age, but here they were on an even keel, soul to soul. Different, but beautiful!

"All you need to do is select the class you want, or the subject you need clarification on, and your Mother or I, or another instructor will be there to assist you," her Father offered. "I had a problem deciding what I wanted to learn, because it seemed there was so much I didn't know. But once in class, I saw that I knew more than I thought I did – or maybe remembered more. It is really a process of remembering."

Christina knew it could be the same for her, but for the moment wanted desperately to be able to communicate with her family on Earth. Her Mother saw a flicker of anxiety in Christina's face and moved to take both her hands in hers and looked into her eyes with that old familiar look, "There is no hurry my dear, you will do it all, and remember "time" is on your side. A little heavenly humor," she added with a chuckle.

Christina hugged them both and turned to leave. Stopping to look over her shoulder at her 'once parents,' she saw them standing hand in hand smiling at her...and standing in front of her old, Earthly, childhood home!

"I do have a lot to learn...or remember."

CHAPTER 29

Emerging from the classroom, Christina had a new sense of who she really was. She felt as though she was a butterfly just released from months of being entrapped in its cocoon. She was beautiful and she could truly fly! It was an enlightening, new kind of freedom. She felt for the first time she could do and be anything she wanted. And it didn't matter where she was! It was a fact whether she was here or in the physical. She was a creator in the purest sense of the word. This was information she wanted desperately to share with her family. If only they could know. What a difference it would make in their lives! This must be how her parents felt while watching her during her struggles on Earth. She hadn't really thought about it that way before. Of course, they watched over her and wanted to help her the same way she was doing with her family. She was so wrapped up in her own objective that she failed to realize others were going through the same thing.

Christina wondered if she was completely oblivious to her Mother's desire to make contact with her. She thought about the times when she felt her Mother's presence and re-called a time when she smelled roses in the kitchen one evening while cooking dinner, even though it was winter and there were no roses about. These must have been signs. Is this what her daughters were experiencing also? Anne has been trying to communicate – is it wishful thinking or does she really hear? Is this what all loved ones go through when they "lose" someone? Why not? Why shouldn't they? Also why shouldn't they communicate? It shouldn't be much different than using a telephone. We are simply in different places and not within eyesight of each other. It's as though your loved one just moved away. No one is really 'dead!' Why is this so hard to understand? Or, rather, why is this so hard to remember?

Christina's mind was in a whirl, jumping from one question to another. Maybe she needed to talk to Sarah and Felicia to become a little more grounded. Laughing at the thought of being grounded in 'heaven,' she decided that perhaps she needed to be 'clouded,' or 'aired.' As if in response to her personal jokes, she heard Sarah's sweet voice, "How about becoming centered!" This was accompanied by Felicia's giggle.

"You rang?" asked Sarah in her smart aleck, imitating-a-butler voice.

"You have been a busy, busy person," Felicia chimed in. Both girls were genuinely pleased to be with Christina again.

"Yes, I guess I have. I saw my grandson! He is so beautiful and his parents are such wonderful parents, and he could see me, and he could hear me, and it was such a happy experience! And now there's going to be a new addition!"

"Hey, slow down there! Now, take a breath and tell us all about it," suggested Sarah, grinning at Christina's exuberance.

"Well, I actually went to see my daughters and Bill, which I did, but I seemed to be visiting at two different times. Which was very confusing to me. First I saw Bill much older and I know he is. Or is he? I just don't know anymore. Then I saw Karen in the kitchen and Scott was hugging her. They were talking about having a baby. Next thing I knew this adorable little boy was running out in the kitchen. I just went to his bedroom to look at him and he saw me! And he could hear me! It was so wonderful to not be cut off from your loved ones, to be seen and heard, just as though I was there in the flesh! It should be that way all the time...why can't it?"

"In more spiritual societies or worlds, it is that way. But Earthly beings are too busy being just that. Earthly. People are not recognizing their own spirituality as the core of who they really are. They still think of themselves as physical bodies housing a spirit, instead of knowing they are spiritual beings who just happen to be using a temporary body. Until this becomes a part of their knowing, only a few will be able to get past the physical limitations they impose on themselves or accept as real," explained Felicia.

Sarah took over, "Yeah, and we all do that in the physical because it is a part of our becoming aware of our true selves. It is a natural step to becoming the spiritual beings we truly are. We must first experience things in the physical in order to know the spiritual. By this I mean really KNOW the spiritual. To know that we are eternal, that we are God, that we are each other, that there are no separations – none! This is a terribly difficult concept for humans to accept. That you and your neighbor are ONE, that you and your enemies are ONE, that you and God are ONE. No separations, no separations, no separations." She looked at Christina with raised eyebrows, nodding her head, as to confirm Christina's understanding.

Christina acknowledged her understanding by nodding back at Sarah gently at first, then smiling and nodding harder and harder, amused at Sarah's fervor. It was as though Sarah was trying to force the information into Christina's knowing with her own intense energy. Christina was realizing just how very much she loved these two friends, teachers and tour guides. She had been so busy, she hadn't given it much thought. But as she did give it thought, it was as though someone had struck a beautiful chord on a piano and it resounded in her as if she were an acoustical chamber of some kind. She felt compelled to tell them of her feelings in that instant.

"I just experienced the most incredible feeling of love for you two and have to tell you how important you are to me and how much I love you."

"You have just experienced what should be experienced on the physical plane. These feelings are the same there, if only people would open up to them and release their fears of rejection, rebuff, the possibility of being hurt or abandoned. They need to learn to put themselves on the line, take the chance, express that love regardless of any and all consequences," said Felicia. "We love you, too!"

It was time to return home and reflect. She knew that the girls knew that she wanted to return to her cottage, and the actual verbalizing wasn't necessary. Hugging each one of the girls, Christina turned and headed toward her place of comfort. As she strolled home she remembered that on her death bed she had the idea that when she died she would miss the trees, flowers, the gentle breezes, the treasures of nature she had come to love so much on her outings with Bill and the girls. She was not willing to give those precious things up. Little did she know. Walking along, she felt the soft breeze, enjoyed the rich, heady aroma of the flowers and trees and became lost in the colors, the likes of which she had never seen duplicated anywhere. There were shades and hues incomparable to anything on Earth. Not only was there nothing to miss, but there was so much more. This is home, not Earth...and she was looking forward to Bill returning home.

She reached her cottage door feeling at peace, happy and anxious for her next adventure.

CHAPTER 30

Having enjoyed her 'time in her cottage reviewing her visits, Christina was planning on contacting Felicia and Sarah, and at the thought, the angel knocker sounded. Knowing it was the girls, she didn't bother to reach out mentally to see who was there, but jumped up and ran to the door. In a little girl way, she decided to put on one of her childhood funny faces when she greeted them. With screwed up face and crossed eyes, she flung open the door. Standing there, instead of the girls, was her beloved brother! Seeing her face he greeted her, "I would have recognized you anywhere! You haven't changed a bit!" With that they both broke up laughing in the way they did when they were children.

Christina threw her arms around him and refused to let go. He returned the hugs and gently pried her arms loose, then held her at arm's length just to look at her. All she could say was, "Why?"

She was referring to the fact that Stephen had left the Earth plane as a young adult, due to excesses with beer and cigarettes. He had had a heart attack and was warned by his physicians that to continue as he was meant an early death. However, should he give up the cigarettes and cut back on the beer, he would be able to reverse the process and go on to live a long life. Christina had gone to be with him in the hospital with his first heart attack and begged him to heed the doctors' advice. He agreed and his wife agreed to help him by doing the same herself. Christina left for home feeling much better about her brother, whom she adored so very much. She couldn't imagine not being able to talk to him, joke with him, and have him as part of her life. He was without a doubt one of the funniest people she had ever known, which even further endeared him to her as she loved a good laugh and often. She could always count on Stephen to do that for her.

After a few months, she discovered that Stephen, in fact, had not followed the doctors' recommendations and had a fatal heart attack at 49 years of age. Having already lost her Mother and Father, Christina just could not accept the fact that Stephen was gone from her life as well. This was impossible! She waited for that phone call, to hear him joke with her or Bill. Bill profoundly felt the loss as well, considering him more a brother than brother-in-law. The four of them, Stephen and Iris, Christina and Bill were very close and spent a lot of time together when they lived in the same town. When Stephen and Iris decided to move out of state, Christina found it very difficult and almost unbearable having them more than a few miles away.

With the acceptance of Stephen's death, Christina became so very angry with him for leaving her and not taking better care of himself to prevent his untimely demise. This was totally unacceptable to her. She found herself yelling at him deciding the louder she yelled, the better he could hear her from wherever he was! Usually a very calm and even-tempered person, she became angry at everyone, even her loving family. She adopted a 'don't get in my way' stance and expected everyone to understand. Which, of course, they did not. Which made her even angrier. She felt as though she was in a time warp from which there was no escape. Her biggest question was, "WHY?" Why so young, why did you leave me, why did you leave your family, why didn't you listen to the doctors, why didn't you stop doing what you were doing? Why? Why? Why?

Staring into Stephen's eyes, she once again asked the question. "Why?"

Understanding the pain she had gone through Stephen held her closer and said, "It was a means to an end. I didn't realize that at the time, of course, but do now. I had completed my journey and fulfilled my planned course for that lifetime, learning and teaching what I went there to do. I

guess I could have chosen another way to leave, but in looking back, this was probably the most painless for everyone
concerned. Including myself. I didn't deserve an agonizing death nor did my loved ones. The concept of 'there are
no accidents,' can sometime be extremely difficult for us to
grasp. I went through what you are going through with Bill.
I visited Iris many time and tried to let her know that I was
okay. In fact, much better than okay – I was wonderful! I
had to get through to her. Unfortunately, I have been unable
to do that. As a result of my Earthly death, she is not taking
care of herself, and has been very ill. As part of the choices
we can make or free will, I believe this is her choice so that
we can be united again. From here I can see that she has a
couple of paths she can follow, and from this vantage point
can see her preferred direction.

"Are you still angry with me?" he said with the old,
familiar twinkle in his eye.

"How could I ever stay mad at you, especially when
you are standing here before me as though you have never
been away!"

"I never was away!"

"Now I know that – but it sure seemed like
it before!"

"Remembering all this, makes me realize even more
what my girls and Bill must be going through. How awful it
must be for them.

"What have you been doing since you have been here?"

"First, I felt I had to keep close watch over Iris and
the boys and was trying very hard to insinuate myself into
their lives, which I found to be impossible very quickly! I
had to learn to watch and not try to control, even though it
was beyond my control. That took a little longer for me being slightly on the stubborn side.

"Spending time with Mom and Dad, I decided to take
some classes, and have enjoyed them immensely. The cur-

rent one is learning different skills to possibly be used in my next lifetime. I will have to make a decision about that. Both when to return and what I would like to have at my disposal as a service to others. That much I did decide on. To be of service. Do I want to be a doctor, or psychic, medium, or naturopathic physician? I just don't know yet, I'm studying all about each one. Having been an EMT last time, I realized that I am moving into a service mode. How many lifetimes for that, I just don't know. But I do feel drawn to it and feel the need to do more next time." Stephen was hesitating and becoming a little pensive.

"You believe you should have gone further with your service before, huh?" asked Christina.

"In my life review, I realized there were areas I was a little lax. I intend to make up for that and unlike before, not quit. Full steam ahead!" With that he smiled a quirky little smile, making a face at Christina.

Christina enjoyed being back with Stephen. She had missed him so very much. It was also such a revelation that nothing is missed. It is always there. The individual, the memories, the humor, the relationship, the emotional ties, the love…especially the love. It is always there! If she had only known! How much grief and anger and sense of loss she could have avoided. She also knew that the grief was necessary in the physical, but to have carried it around for so long probably was not necessary.

Stephen was preparing to leave and said, "It's so good to have you near again, Sis. I have a class to attend and will expect to see you there soon! You need to get with the program, and quit dilly-dallying around!!" With that he kissed her cheek and left. He didn't walk away – he just left!

CHAPTER 31

Staring at the empty doorway, Christina thought, "Just like him! Let's not do anything the ordinary way." As she turned around, thinking she would sit at her piano for a while, perched in front of the bench, were Cookie and Ling. Surprised, she asked, "What are you two doing here?"

Without knowing how, she heard them communicating with her in language she could understand. They were asking her to accompany them and it was important. "Lead the way," she said.

The animals headed out the still open door in the normal way and she followed. They led her to a tunnel which was brilliant with light. Immediately she remembered more detail of her transition. "I remember having been here! I came through here when I left Bill and the hospital bed! I remember! I lifted up off the bed and looked back at Bill, who was cradling me in his arms and crying, and the girls were standing with their husbands next to the bed. I felt the pull toward him and the girls, but there was a stronger pull toward this tunnel. I hovered above wanting to comfort them, but at the same time feeling free and healed and unencumbered. Finally the pull to this tunnel was too strong and I left my beloved family and the hospital room.

"I saw my parents and Stephen, grandparents, friends and Angelic Beings all along the way. And you two! I saw you two there as well! The next thing I remember is waking with all the wonderful people around me."

Both Cookie and Ling looked up at her, reinforcing her recollections.

Suddenly, she realized she must be here to be there for someone coming over. For a split second she panicked! "Who is coming over? Is it Bill? Anne? Karen? Who?" Cookie and Ling sat down at Christina's feet as though to wait. Christina looked down the tunnel to see a very small figure approach...wagging its tail!

"It's Tippy! Tippy, Tippy, come here, sweet boy!"

Tippy ran up to her and sniffed at Cookie and Ling, with Cookie wagging in response and Ling rubbing up against him. So excited to see Tippy, it momentarily skipped Christina's mind that Bill must be grieving the loss of his close companion. Realizing her selfish attitude, she was overcome with guilt feelings.

Instantly, Josef appeared by her side. "Let go of those feelings immediately," he said lovingly. "You have done nothing wrong. You are naturally happy to see Tippy. He needed you here, and to be happy to see him! You will be able to send Bill the loving thoughts he will need to heal. Enjoy your reunion!" With that Josef became his familiar, beautiful ball of light and sped off, leaving Christina feeling calm and free of anxiety.

Tippy took a great leap and landed in Christina's arms, which made her giggle with a feeling of lightness and joy. As she hugged him, he began licking, covering her entire face! Laughing, she held him out from her and looked in his face and he smiled at her. What a reunion! She put him down and he pranced in front of her between Cookie and Ling and the four happy Beings headed for her cottage.

Christina and the three animals settled into her sofa content with the nearness of one another. Inwardly Christina knew they would not be staying here with her, but how she knew, she did not know. Maybe she had heard there was a special place in heaven for the animals where they could roam free, playing with each other, running through meadows and trees. Whatever the case, she took it as fact; therefore she was not surprised when the three moved toward her front door. The door opened, without her help, and they bid her farewell - temporarily, of course, because she knew they would be back. She reminded herself that at some time she wanted to visit the place of the animals. She hadn't really thought about that before and could only imagine what it must be like. "I'll mention this to Sarah and Felicia."

CHAPTER 32

It occurred to Christina that Bill must be awfully lonely without Tippy and could almost feel his distress. It was time to revisit her loved one and try to console him. Too many losses. Or what he would consider a loss. She prepared herself for her trip and sent a thought to Josef, just in case she needed him to get back. "Covering all bases," she thought to herself.

"You are doing well," she heard.

She arrived at her Earthly home and found Bill working in the back yard digging holes for the Spring bulbs. It must be Fall as she and Bill enjoyed shopping for the different colors and varieties each year. Bill was far better at this than she was, but she sure enjoyed the Spring bloom! He was wearing a heavy cardigan sweater, which was well-used and one that Christina had begged him repeatedly to give to charity. Obviously, he still refused to part with it, even though it now hung on him loosely, making him appear even more thin than he had actually become. He seemed a lot thinner and gaunt looking to Christina. "Is this from grieving?" she asked herself aloud. She moved closer to him and was amazed to discover he was thin of hair which was nearly all white, with mustache to match. His face, full of character, was now accompanied by a lot more wrinkles as his skin hung loosely in areas previously endowed with muscle.

"Not grieving, but age! How long has it been? I've been busy, but it seems as though only a couple of days or weeks. This is difficult to get used to! I wonder how old Tippy was when he joined me. How old is Bill? So many questions, so few answers!"

The white orb appeared over her right shoulder and bounced as if trying to get her attention. Josef didn't bother taking a human-like form, but instead maintained his golden glow, albeit, one that spoke.

"You are confused, because you are trying to put the situation into a linear time capsule as you had experienced on Earth. It does not work that way here, or actually anywhere, it just appears that way. Watch!" Josef commanded. With that the sphere bounced over to Bill and although he was still working in the yard, he now filled out his sweater in the way Christina remembered, even though the sweater was still not much improved! Bill, younger than when she first arrived, was still older than when she left him.

"You are visiting Bill at a time-line you desired, because of your wish to have him with you. It was a subconscious thing on your part, because it was completely unintentional. Let go of your idea to have him with you and he will fall into a more 'physically logical' frame of reference. Everything happens at the same time. You are just 'popping in' at a time closer to his reuniting with you on the other side. You are not actually changing anything – it is just your perception of it."

Still finding the concept confusing, Christina thanked Josef, determined to attend one of those classes to better understand how it all functioned.

Watching Bill work, she also noticed a small mound under the tree they both planted together to commemorate their new home, which was now quite tall and full of Fall color. At the head of the mound was a small, wooden placard lovingly etched with the name, "Tippy." She knew Bill had taken the time to put Tippy's name in the wood and that it had been a labor of love. Bill moved over to the mound as Christina watched, and dug a small shallow hole then placed a few bulbs there for their beloved pet.

"There you go, boy! Now you will be beautiful in the Spring." Bill smiled at the small mound and went back to the rest of his gardening. Feeling a presence, Christina looked down and there wagging his tail in complete approval was Tippy. As a sudden realization, Christina knew that

Tippy had returned at that moment because Bill had spoken to him with love in his heart for the little guy. This is what drew Tippy to him. Bill was handling it quite well.

CHAPTER 33

Turning to Tippy, Christina said, "Show me where you are living now."

In what would be considered a 'blink of an eye,' they were standing in the middle of a rolling meadow with every imaginable animal present. They were in complete accord with no animosity, no predator, no prey, no jealousy, just comradeship. There were people playing with their pets, with balls and frizbees in the air, and cats and kittens playing with each other. This area was full of domestic animals, but also wild birds that were usually seen in back yards at bird feeders, squirrels, rabbits, chipmunks, all at peace with one another. So natural! Christina realized they were here by choice as well as in the area of her cottage. Obviously they are free to move about, but this is their home.

Felicia and Sarah appeared at her side just as she was marveling at the sight before her.

"I have always heard of 'animal heaven" but never really thought about what it would be," Christina told her friends. "I have so many questions."

Ahead of them there appeared to be a couple of puppies frolicking and jumping up at something unseen. They were heading toward the three girls. As they approached, another ball of light appeared and dissolved into a Being. Wearing a long robe, he had birds around him, a squirrel on his shoulder and holding a rabbit. Right out of Walt Disney, Christina thought, looking for all the world like St. Francis of Assisi! As the thought was formulated, the Being introduced himself as Seth.

"I heard all your questions, and will answer them the best I can. With your Earthly limitations, it may be difficult for you to completely comprehend, but you can certainly get the overview.

"Animals belong to group souls moving from the wild to domestic Beloved pets having been nurtured, cared for, protected and loved, eventually will begin their individual process of evolution breaking away from the group, thanks to the help of the human species. How many times have you heard 'he/she doesn't know he/she is a dog/cat?' It is a beginning step to individuation. These are the ones leaving the animal side and visiting your home, coming and going as they please. They will come back to you many times on the Earth plane, often several times in your one lifetime, in the forms of different pets. You may notice certain similar traits being exhibited and carried over from one pet to the next. Reminders of who they were or are. Their way of letting you know they are not gone. You have formed a loving bond that is repeated over and over.

Not much difference between animal and human kingdoms, huh?"

Taking all this in, Christina became aware of both Ling and Tippy calmly sitting at her feet looking up at her, reinforcing the loving bond they had all created together. Seth continued, "There is another area for you to see, although it may be difficult to comprehend."

The new area appeared to be jungle and Christina headed in that direction with Tippy at her heels. Every imaginable jungle animal was living there, again in perfect accord with each other. A closer look revealed some people actually walking among the lions, elephants and tigers.

"I don't know if I am ready for that yet!" Christina said to Tippy. Tippy gave her that 'all knowing' look as if to say, nothing can hurt you here!

"I know that Tippy! But it is still something I have to get used to. Guess I carried some of those old belief systems over here with me. In time, I will definitely give it a try…just not right now! I must admit it is a beautiful sight to see.

"What about the marine life?"

With that comment, Seth transported them all to a beautiful sea so clear you could see to the bottom. Within it were all kinds of fish. The dolphins and whales were together, playing tag with the seals.

"It is so obvious that all things are loved and it is so beautiful to see!"

Seth said, "This is the way it was intended to be and will be again, once mankind realizes the gifts at their fingertips. Man was meant to be guardians of the animals and was given dominion, which means to care for, nurture and love, not to dominate and kill. A slight misinterpretation of the intention!"

Christina and the girls thanked Seth for his guided tour and beautiful information. He bowed slightly and moved into the ball of light followed by the romping puppies jumping up at his unseen robes.

CHAPTER 34

Christina left Tippy and headed back to her place of comfort to reflect, once again, on all her new-found information. "An awful lot of reflecting going on!" She thought to herself. It seemed to her that this was the original plan for Earth...for every living thing to co-exist in harmony with each other. What changed? How did it become what it is today? And when? And why? Again, so many questions and so few answers. Somehow Christina knew that there were a lot of answers that would not be revealed to her. At least not this time around.

She thought to herself, "Everyone and everything is so well taken care of, no matter where we are temporarily residing. When in the physical it is almost impossible to imagine the 'no accident' theory, the 'no wrong' theory, the idea of good vs. bad being real. But here you can see that all and everything is truly in Divine Order!

"Before I take any classes I believe I will go to the library and pick out books that will enlighten me about what happened on Earth to change what was evidently part of the original plan. And most importantly, what can we do to correct the mistakes we have made."

She no sooner completed her thought, when several books appeared in her own library covering every conceivable issue that was bugging her.

Visualizing a cup of tea, it appeared in her hand, as she settled into the deep sofa with a couple of chosen books and began to read. It soon became clear that no mistakes had actually been made, but that it just simply was. There are no mistakes and everything can be made whole and beautiful through the minds of man. Everything can and will live in harmony ultimately. This is all part of the experience, the growing, the enlightenment, the being, that we all must go through.

She also realized that in some cases, just by placing her hands on the book, she could assimilate much of its content. Therefore, she was well into her third book when there was a knock at her door.

CHAPTER 35

Opening her door she saw standing before her, her brother Stephen, his usual impish grin, warming her heart. They hugged, just enjoying each other's presence.

"I came to talk with you about something important to me," Stephen announced.

"You can talk with me anytime, not just when it is important! What's going on?"

"I have come to a decision about being here. I believe it is time for me to return to Earth."

"What? You just got here! Why are you thinking of leaving? What are you going to do?"

"I have been checking on opportunities for me if I return. We do get to make those choices you know. I can now fulfill some of the things I had attempted to do before and never completed. I was an Emergency Tech and now I see a chance for me to involve myself in the new medical field. A field in which there is so much being done in the natural way, moving away from the synthetics, with more of the hands on approach, using Earth's bounty, rather than chemicals. It is so exciting for me to watch. I could be a healer in the truest sense of the word! It is all moving in that direction now."

Christina, feeling a little stunned by the idea, sat and picked up her almost empty teacup. "We just haven't had much time together and I will miss you again!"

"No you won't! I will still be here with you. I will come back every night during sleep, and maybe even by then you will have developed your abilities to see and talk to me from here. Plus in the early years, I will be back here more often than not. I will, of course, watch over the baby-body and take care of it, but can also do a lot of that from here. I won't be spending 100% of my time in body as a baby. I'll just 'supervise,' so to speak." With that he laughed and tried to make light of leaving his sister again. "I have been watching our Aunt and Uncle, who have already returned and are now newly-weds and will be expecting a child soon. That child could be me, should I decide to accept this mission," he said jokingly.

Trying to keep the apprehensive tone from her voice, Christina said, "It all sounds wonderful for you. I'll just miss you, that's all. I also remember how close we all were as a family before, with our Aunt and Uncle practically as second parents, so it would almost be a natural transition for you. This is all just something I have not really given any thought to before now. I guess it needs to be thought about though, at some time. I'm just not ready for it."

"Of course, you are not ready for it. You have not been here as long as I have. Also, since I left Earth early, I have an opportunity to return more quickly. Stay as long as you like!" he said jokingly, as he waved his hand across her room as a king surveying his kingdom. "Anyway, I am still investigating it and have not made the final decision yet. I still have some time, but I will keep you posted. I just wanted to tell you about it and maybe get some input from you. But I can tell you are not exactly ready for this yet. But I'm patient!" With that he went to her front door, bowed a formal bow, and left. He was much more adept at these things than she was.

"Going back. Humph, that is not something that I have even considered yet. Maybe some day, but I am certainly in no big hurry, if ever!"

CHAPTER 36

Just the thought of going back brought Bill and the girls to mind and Christina felt the tug back to them. Giving into the tug, she found herself standing next to Bill, who was talking on the phone to Anne.

"Anne, I am feeling awfully tired these days and just don't accomplish the things I set out to do! I tire too quickly. Sometimes my legs feel like lead weights. I was in the garden today at Tippy's grave I swear I felt Mom's presence. Even after all this time I miss her so much and little Tippy too! Enough about me, how is little Ashley?"

"Ashley is fine, Dad. Quit trying to change the subject. You are going to be fine – you just need to rest more and take care of yourself. Are you taking your vitamins?"

"Yeah, yeah. Now you are sounding just like your Mother. I take them and all the other stuff the Doctor gave me. Sometimes I think all that junk does more harm than good. I am just tired, that's all."

"Do you want me to come over? Are you alright?"

"Quit worrying about me, I am just fine! I told you I am only tired."

"Okay, but if you need me…CALL."

"I will."

"Promise?"

"Promise."

With that he hung up.

Christina realized that something was going on here, but was not quite sure what. Bill did look older and thinner and wondered if this was created by her desire to be with him or was he actually older and thinner. She watched him as he crossed the room and flopped into his favorite chair and let out a big sigh as if he was exhausted. This had nothing to do with vitamins or medicines or just being tired. Something more was going on. He sat with his eyes closed and looked as if he had fallen asleep quickly. Christina reached out and stroked his forehead and his eyelids fluttered very slightly, but enough that she noticed. The love and concern she felt for this man was overwhelming.

Right then Christina made the decision to go talk to Anne, since she seemed to be open to receiving messages from her, and tell her about her Father's change. At the thought, she was standing in Anne's living room where Anne was just hanging up the phone from talking with her Father. She was looking a bit agitated.

Anne turned to John with an apprehensive look on her face, which John noticed instantly. "What's going on? Is Dad okay?"

"I am not sure. All I know is he is not himself lately and he has me worried. He's just so tired all the time. Maybe the correct word is 'exhausted.' I know it will be next to impossible to get him to a doctor, but I feel I should push it and take him there myself if necessary."

"I know how stubborn he can be and if you want me to come with you to talk with him, I will."

Anne moved over to John and threw her arms around him and gave him a big hug.

"You are always there for me when I need you and I want you to know how much I appreciate it and love you!" John smiled hugging her back, "I am always there for you and always will be. First thing in the morning we will go and see Dad."

Christina stood looking at her daughter and glanced past her to the kitchen where her granddaughter Ashley sat doing homework. She reminded Christina so much of her brother, with her strawberry blonde curls framing a pixie face. She was working so intently, and surprisingly, without prompting and coercing from her parents. She was actually enjoying her homework! Darling and smart. What a great combination. Not at all surprising considering her parents, and of course, her grandparents!

Having seen and heard Anne and Scott's conversation Christina felt her concern for Bill dissipate and it was replaced with the knowledge that everything was okay and taken care of. Her family was in charge. Her wonderful family. She nodded a goodbye to all three and left.

CHAPTER 37

Hearing the doctor's words sent shivers of shock through Anne. Even though you know it is inevitable, you still want to believe it won't happen to you or your family...ever! Christina stood by in the corner of Doctor Milner's office and watched her beloved Bill as the doctor told him that after a review of all the tests, he had congestive heart failure which was advanced enough that there was little they could do for him other than make him comfortable. Bill accepted the information with a calm presence and a kind of resignation. Christina knew that he had already expected as much, but never wanted to voice it, especially to his daughters. No need to worry them unnecessarily.

Tears appeared in Anne's eyes and managed a path down her cheek as John put his arm around her shoulder in an effort to comfort her, lending as much support as possible. This was going to be difficult for the girls, especially after losing their Mother when they were so young. It is always hard to lose a parent no matter what their age or yours.

Even though Bill was still able to mostly take care of himself, Dr. Milner suggested he be admitted to hospice.

Anne literally jerked at the sound of the word. "He's not dying is he? Look at him! He's walking, talking, even cooking for himself!"

Dr. Milner explained a person does not have to be completely incapacitated to be on hospice, that the prerequisite was a diagnosis of 6 months or less life expectancy and that he could be on hospice and stay at home.

"I can be there for him without hospice! I can take care of him." Anne was nearly shouting.

Bill tried to calm her down, when Dr. Milner interrupted saying, "Hospice will send a nurse around on a regular basis to check on your Father, a nursing assistant to help with some of his personal hygiene when necessary, a Social

Worker to help with the insurance, finances and funeral arrangements if needed. They can also supply a Chaplain and a Volunteer if Bill so chooses. Don't look at this as the end of everything. In many cases it prolongs the life and most certainly provides comfort and security to the patient and family. It definitely improves the quality of life of the patient. I am not asking you to make a decision right this minute, but I would ask you, Bill, to contact this hospice and talk with them. Interview them, if you will. Then you can make an educated decision." With that Dr. Milner handed them a brochure for their review.

As they left the doctor's office, Bill could still see that Anne was fighting the entire idea and also struggling with the chore of telling Karen and Scott. Bill put his arm around Anne, hugging her and said, "This is not bad at all and I want to be the one to tell Karen since I can see you are wrestling with this. I'll call the hospice and talk with them and let you know what I decide. I only wish we had considered this with your Mom. Can you imagine what a help that would have been?"

Anne nodded reluctantly, knowing she had already lost any argument they may have had about this. She also knew that he was looking at being reunited with her Mom, although she was not going to verbalize this knowledge. Saying it makes it more real, somehow.

Christina followed them out of the office and was so pleased with the way it had been handled by the doctor. She also knew that Anne and Karen would be pleasantly surprised with the care their Father would receive. Since the girls both lived close by, they would be checking on Bill frequently then eventually on a daily basis. Knowing everything was taken care of and feeling relieved, Christina left for home. It was strange realizing that she was not "needed" in the same way as before. She thought to herself, "Mothers are always needed, are they not?"

CHAPTER 38

Arriving in the comfort of her home and her special couch, Christina stretched out and thought about her daughters. Anne, the take charge kind of person she was and capable of overseeing the well-being of the rest of the family, would be in her element. Karen, always the happy spirit, 'everything is going to be okay,' will lend the perfect balance to the family situation. They would all be fine. She mentally embraced each one, daughters, son-in-laws, grandchildren and her beautiful Bill. All so special and loving and competent. She had been blessed with them all in her life. Especially those little ones who came in her after-life, and would make an impact in their world.

She decided it was time to find her own Mother and Father and tell them about what was going on and share her feelings of joy with them.

Find had nothing to do with it. The thought alone brought them to her door. Still creating the surprise in Christina, as she wondered if she would every get used to it. They embraced one another with the aura of love surrounding them. Christina started to tell them of what was happening with her family, and of course, they already knew.

"We still keep tabs on the goings-on with our family. The ties and very strong," her Mother explained. "We also know that everything is in order and will be divinely directed by Bill and by Karen and Anne."

"I know this, but for some reason, I felt concern for the situation."

Christina's Father reached out to her and taking her hand said, "That's a normal reaction, which will be replaced by your 'knowing' instead. You are still somewhat attached, so to speak, to your family, experiencing those Earthly concerns, which in reality are not real! Sometimes a hard concept to grasp, but one that you will come to understand completely."

Her Mother had to add, "Now you can see what your Father and I went through when it was you facing your mortality and what you had to go through. We still wanted to take away the suffering and the pain. But we had help in understanding that it was all according to a divine plan, you yourself had laid out for yourself! Just as we are helping you understand now. We are all here for each other and it is a constant learning experience in all phases of life and Life."

"All I can say is I am glad you are here for me now. So when I fall back on my old thinking patterns, I will come to you to straighten me out!"

Her Mother couldn't resist, "Yes, we are still straightening you out! Anytime you want us, just call. We'll come running, so to speak. We must be off now and we love you."

With that, they were gone as quickly as they had appeared. "How do they do that?" Christina thought to herself.

Then she heard that familiar voice, "It's easy. You do it yourself, you just don't realize it." She turned around to see the ball of light bouncing around her. "Okay, Josef, show yourself!"

As he deliberately and slowly took the form that Christina was used to seeing, he said, "Looks as though you have had yourself a very busy day. How are you feeling about it all?"

"I guess I am getting used to the idea that all the things people experience on the Earth plane are of their own choosing, although sometimes a little difficult to accept. This was part of their life plan all along."

"Imagine how they feel about accepting the fact they chose this for themselves," Joseph suggested.

"I remember wanting to argue with people when they told me I created the situation. It is just much harder to accept there than it is here, where you can see the bigger picture. Seeing what is happening there right now, I would love to tell them and show them the bigger picture instead of them struggling so."

"But then you would be robbing them of the experience. The experience which is part of their divine plan for themselves. You wouldn't want to do that would you?"

"Of course not!" Christina answered.

"I knew you would feel that way! I know that you now understand that what you went through was of your own choosing as well. Was it not?"

"Difficult as it was, yes, I see now that it was part of my overall plan. But you know I still feel some grief over it when I see my family suffering. I truly wish people could understand that their prolonged grieving affects us here. Of course, it is natural for people to grieve and it is also very necessary, but to fall into it and allow it to become a part of their lives is disheartening and it was not meant to be that way. If they only knew more about us over here and what we are doing, they would, in fact, be joyful and happy for us and I almost believe somewhat envious!"

"Isn't it amazing what we begin to understand from a totally different perspective? I would imagine you would not have felt that way when you were on the Earth plane, am I correct?"

"You are absolutely right! I did my fair share of grieving. Except now I find myself grieving for them from this perspective. Is there a difference?"

"No, not much. The difference being they don't feel your grief the same as you feel theirs, as they are not as open. Plus they are not seeing as you are seeing. But please remember, there is some overflow from you to them, whether they are aware of it or not. I know there were times, when you "felt" your Mother's presence when you were going through your difficult time of loss. This was her grieving for your suffering. So on some level you were picking her up."

"Gosh, I didn't realize. I guess I had better be careful. I sure don't want to add anything negative to what they are going through. It just proves to me how connected to each other we really are.

"Thanks, Josef, for setting me straight."

"There is no 'setting straight' it is just a reminder and a new awareness. Besides, as you know, it is my pleasure."

With that he shimmered and became the beautiful orb of light once again and simply 'bounced' away.

"It is definitely going to be a while before I get used to that," Christina thought to herself.

"In due time my dear, in due time," she heard as a light chuckle moved off into the distance.

CHAPTER 39

There was that need again. Christina felt it was time to revisit Bill and see what was happening. Instantly, she found herself standing beside their old, shared bed and saw that Bill was sleeping. She leaned over him and whispered his name. With that, Bill looked up, sat up, and lifted out of his body to greet her.

"Together again," she whispered to him. "I came to get you and take you someplace really special for a visit."

"So I am not dead?" Bill responded.

"No, but it is somewhat similar," Christina said with her usual adoring look aimed directly at Bill.

Bill smiled at her, "Okay, I am putty in your hands, lead on beautiful wife!"

Christina took his hand and they lifted up and out of the house into the beautiful moonlit and star-filled sky, passing over Anne's and Karen's homes, for a quick reassurance all was well within.

She guided Bill to her 'home.' "I wanted you to see this and a little of where I have been spending my time waiting for you." Just for fun and because she loved it so much, she reached up and used the angel knocker on her door. The door simply opened.

He looked around at all the comforts and thought about taking a tour, when Christina pointed out there was nothing more to see. "I don't need a kitchen, bathroom, or any of the extra rooms we had on Earth. If I want a salad, I would just create it rather than fix it in the kitchen. Oh, I could if I wanted, but I decided, 'Why?' I'll leave that to the chefs that couldn't get enough of it on Earth!"

Bill smiled at her and said, "But I see you still have a fireplace – you surely don't need that!"

"No, of course not. It is just one of those comforts of home that we had together and I was not ready to part with it, nor did I have to. This is my home and I created everything you see here. I can change it any time I wish, but so far I like it just as it is. I wanted to share this with you so you could see what is ahead for you. Mom and Dad and Stephen are here and many others. Bill, this is home! This is where we come from and this is where we return to. Isn't it wonderful?"

"I do believe it is wonderful. Will I create my own home when I get here? Or can we share?" Bill was looking a little concerned.

"Sweetheart, we can do whatever we want – that is the beauty of it. We are not tied into anything, especially anything we don't want. And it is all done by agreement. Isn't that exciting?

"Come on, let's take a walk. We'll talk along the way." Christina took Bill's hand and led him to her array of flowers in front of her home. "I wanted to show you where you will be coming soon. Although you are not seeing it as I see it or hearing it as I hear it, you can still see how beautiful it is." Creating the river they would walk by in the evenings together, Christina could see the young Bill she had fallen in love with as he admired the river and felt the cool air it offered.

"I have missed you, Christina." He put his arm around her and held her tight.

"I have missed you as well, but I also wanted to show you how things are here and that I am truly happy, safe and waiting for your return. I am hoping you will be able to retain this memory when you awaken. Things are wonderful here and there is absolutely nothing to fear. It is a shame we have spent so much time fearing something this beautiful. Maybe you can share this experience with the girls as well when you get back.

"When you come home to me we should take time to re-create our new home together and maybe even put it next to a river. There's someone else I need for you to see before you go back."

Instantly, Tippy appeared at Bill's side with tail wagging and his usual jumping, happy to see his friend, companion and Daddy. Bill reached down and picked Tippy up and enjoyed every lick and kiss he received. "I have missed you too, big boy! I guess this means we will be together again as well. I see your Mom has been taking good care of you since you left me." More kisses with a little nuzzling of Bill's neck.

Christina took him from Bill and gave him a hug and put him down. "See? Nothing really changes, it just gets better. There is so much more, but we don't have the time – well, I have the time – all I want, but you don't. I can see you are beginning to fade a little which means you are preparing to wake up. Take my hand and I will escort you back to our, or your, bedroom. Just try to remember at least some of this when you wake up. It will make things much easier for you. Also remember I am here waiting for you and I love you."

She hugged him and Bill offered her his hand and Christina gently led him back to his Earthly home and bed. She watched him gently slide into his sleeping body. She blew him a kiss and left for home.

CHAPTER 40

Bill awoke feeling something important had happened during the night. He lay very still trying to remember his dream. Bits and pieces of it came to him and he knew it involved Christina. There was a house...a beautiful house, but at the same time a funny house because it had no kitchen, no bathrooms and was just a one-room house. Weird! Then for some reason he thought of Tippy buried in the back yard with the garden planted around him and a dream of Tippy and gardens came to him. Vividly colored gardens and a very happy Tippy. As he lay there trying to remember more, he could have sworn he caught a whiff of Christina's perfume, although he didn't think there was any of it left in the house any more. He had to admit to himself that he felt a lot closer to her than he had in a while and also discovered he wouldn't be at all surprised to see Tippy jump up on the bed, tail wagging! "Something must have happened," he thought to himself. "Something important, something I am supposed to remember."

Throughout Bill's day, bits and pieces of his adventure started coming back to him. He would see something or hear something that would tweak his memory and tease him into remembering one more little piece. "I know I was with Christina and she was showing me something. There was beauty and I have a good feeling about it when I think about it. I also keep picturing a fireplace. What on earth would that have to do with anything? If I could just pull it all together."

As it happened, by the end of the day, Bill was able to piece together all his short rememberings and get a pretty complete picture of what happened. He also knew that this was not actually a dream, because he could still 'feel' Christina, feel her touch, her embrace, her love. And Tippy. What a joy that was. "I know I held him as I can still feel the warmth of his little body in my arms and his wet kisses," Bill told himself out loud.

"I need to call the girls and ask them over to tell them of this experience. I know that is what Christina would want."

Reaching for the phone Bill sat in his chair and called Anne first telling her he had some important information for her and her sister. Of course, Anne tried to drag it out of him on the phone, "What is it Dad, what is going on, are you okay?"

"Typical, concerned Anne," Bill thought to himself and he called Karen. "Sure Dad, what time do you want us?"

"Just anytime after dinner would be fine. I'll see you both then! I love you!"

Hanging up the phone, Bill thought about how he was going to deliver this news to all of them without sounding as though he had lost his mind along with his health. He knew the time was getting close, he could just feel it, so he knew he could not waste time in telling them the good news. At least what he considered good news. Of course, they may not think of it that way at all. So be it. He will do what he can.

CHAPTER 41

Sarah and Felicia were sitting on a hill overlooking a lovely valley and for fun creating visuals for one another. Felicia would pop up a tree here and Sarah would place a squirrel in the tree and added a white fence around it. Felicia put a bluebird on a fence post and not to be outdone, Sarah imagined a raccoon napping under the fence. Both very pleased with their game and giggling at each other, Felicia said, "Maybe it needs a hippo on the other side of the fence." They leaned back on their elbows admiring their handiwork when they heard the soft voice (or thought) coming from Christina. Smiling at each other, they stood, erasing their created scene, they held hands and appeared on Christina's doorstep.

"Guess she needs us," Felicia said.

"Well, she has been busy lately," said Sarah as she reached for the angel knocker. Before she even had time to lift it, Christina opened the door.

"I knew you would come, so I created some tea for all of us, and while we all sit together, I will tell you what has been going on with me and my family." Christina proceeded to fill her friends in on all the happenings with Bill and her daughters and how she went to see Bill and brought him home for a visit. "I guess that's all right, especially since no one stopped me."

Sarah smiled and said, "Of course, it's all right! This is his home too! Did you have a nice visit?"

"Well, yes. I just wasn't able to really show him, if you know what I mean. There seemed to be limits to what he could see and hear. But I do believe he saw and experienced enough to alleviate any fears he may have had, and that was the main idea of bringing him here. I just wish we could tell everyone so there would be less grieving and fear associated with dying. Why can't that be?"

Hearing the frustration in Christina's voice, Felicia reached out for her hand and said, "Stop and think about what you have learned here, or should I say 'remembered' here, and I believe you can answer your own question."

"You are right, I know. I just want to save them from their unknowing, or lack of knowledge, or mis-guided information placed before them by religions, and the guilt-producing fears. Is that so wrong?"

"Of course not! It is just your compassion and loving-nature getting in the way of allowing your loved ones their own paths. You already know we all end up at the same place and in our own proper time and method. If it had not been right for Bill to come here with you, it would not have happened the way it did. It may have taken more effort on his part, to be a willing participant. However, it is obvious he was ready for this intervention on your part. Just remember, all these decisions are theirs to make, not ours or anyone else's." Felicia sat back and watched Christina and could almost see the acceptance settle in and the understanding appear in her eyes.

"We find it hard to let go of ideas and things on Earth, and I guess it is sometimes just as hard here, until we completely accept the knowledge that everything is truly in Divine Order. I knew I needed you both here to keep me in line and set me straight."

They both smiled at Christina, remembering their own process when they arrived here and the adjustments that were made until they remembered. Always learning. But forever patient until you do.

Sarah reminded her, "There is no time line to any of this, and you are not being graded in any way - it just is whenever and however. Isn't it nice that there is no time and no grades? As a teacher, you had enough of that on Earth, right?"

"Indeed, I did!"

Stephen knocked on Christina's door. When she opened it he stepped in greeting Sarah and Felicia and said to his sister, "Let's talk."

CHAPTER 42

Left alone, Stephen said, "I want to show you something." He showed her to the couch where they both sat. As if on a movie screen, there appeared before them a scene of a young married couple. It was obvious the wife was very much pregnant and seemed to be in some discomfort. Her anxious husband was escorting her to the car with suitcase in hand. Christina and Stephen sat and watched the activity unfold before them.

Stephen turned to look at Christina without saying anything, waiting for some kind of reaction. She turned to her brother and asked, "What is this? Who is this? What is going on?"

Stephen smiled and said, "I am getting ready to leave here. For a while I will be back to see you regularly, until my Earth existence allows me to forget...or maybe not, but in any case for a while I can be in both places. At least until the complete transition has been made. That couple you are seeing is our last-life's aunt and uncle and that baby they are about to deliver, will be me. I have made the decision to go back a fulfill some of the intentions of my last life. Please be happy for me for this is what I want to do."

Christina was in a mild state of shock, not having thought that far ahead to what may be. "Stephen, if this is what you want, then it is what I want for you. You will just have to come back and tell me what it was like and I will check in on you from time to time. I will miss you."

"I doubt that you will. Probably at some point you will return as well and we will be together again in some capacity. Maybe friends, maybe relatives, but the choice will be yours. We have been together before and will be again. Remember that, and also remember that I love you!"

"I love you too!"

"Medical profession, here I come! Look out world!"

With that, in his usual fashion, he just disappeared along with the movie screen.

"Wow!" Christina said. "He never was one for 'good-byes'!"

CHAPTER 43

Christina was walking among her flowers in front of her cottage admiring the brilliant colors unmatched on Earth, and the different sounds that coordinated with each different fragrance. As she touched the petals their music increased as if speaking to her. She wondered if they did this on Earth and we were just not open to hearing them. She imagined they did. Among her thoughts, she heard another melodic voice softly singing and thought it sounded familiar. She stopped and listened, tuning into it and realized it was the lovely voice of Anne she was hearing. Then joining was the softer voice of Karen. At that moment she felt the distinctive pull, the familiar pull that was Bill's and she allowed herself to be drawn away from her garden to join her Earthly family.

She arrived at the bedside of her husband in their bedroom with Bill appearing to be sleeping. Anne and Karen were on either side of him each holding a hand. Their attentive husbands were standing behind them lending support. Anne and Karen were softly singing to their Father.

Christina noticed the orbs of light moving around the room and knew who they were. There were many and she supposed they were the angels of the rest of the family as well as the ones there for Bill. Off to her side, she recognized one very special ball of light bouncing toward her, and in his shimmering way Josef appeared briefly, sending his love and smiling at her to let her know he was there for her if needed. Christina nodded her acknowledgment and thanks and Josef shimmered away. She thought to herself, "Lots and lots of help filling this room."

Christina leaned over and kissed Bill on the forehead, when he lifted out of his body and went to her side. They both looked at his waning body, lovingly cared for by their children. Bill was amazed at what he saw, not ever remembering seeing himself from a distance in this way. He saw colorful lights around his family, but noticed the lights around his body were not as bright and seemed to be somewhat washed out.

Bill kissed Christina's ear and asked, "Am I dead?"

"No, my dearest, not yet, but as you can see the time is near. As you can also see, it will be easy, no suffering and quite beautiful. What more could you ask for than to be sung over to the other side surrounded by love and caring! It was their lovely voices that carried me here to your side."

Arms around each other, Christina and Bill watched their daughters and sons-in-law, all with tears on their cheeks, sending their Father on his way, albeit somewhat hesitantly, but knowingly.

Bill said, "We were so blessed with these girls and blessed again that they found the husbands they did. Our grandchildren are very special too. I wish you could have known them."

"Oh, but I did! I have watched over all of you for such a long time. I have seen that Andrew and Ashley will grow into fine young adults and have been in touch with them both."

The hospice nurse had been called and at that point she came into the room to check on Bill and see how his family was doing. She asked the girls to accompany her into the hallway to tell them that it could be any time now. "His vital signs are decreasing, his breathing is shallow and irregular, and his color is graying. I would recommend staying here for a while."

The girls nodded, but they already knew and had every intention of staying with their Father.

Christina looked at Bill, leaned over and kissed him on the cheek, "I have to go now, but I will be there waiting for you."

Bill smiled at her lovingly, and as they both looked at the failing body they saw a hint of a smile appear on his face. He slowly and unwillingly moved back to his body as Christina waved to him and disappeared.

Both girls looked at each other as they saw the smile appear and nodded. Scott and John asked what that was all about and they both said, "Dad just saw Mom. She was just here to help him cross."

All four held hands reaching across Bill's failing body and sang softly together to usher their beloved Father to his new world.

CHAPTER 44

Christina heard the music announcing Bill's arrival and went to meet him. As he came through that tunnel of light she was waiting for him along with many others from his busy life. Among them were the angels and guides that stood by him and helped through the difficult times. Bill headed straight into Christina's arms and they embraced long and hard.

She took his hand and they headed for her, or rather, their cottage. She stopped to show him the garden and to appreciate the color, feel and sound before moving into their comfortable living room.

She showed him how to make a cup of tea, by holding out his hands and picturing the cup he wanted filled with his favorite kind.

So much to do, so many places to go, so many people to meet. So much time. She knew he would be in awe about so much, as she was.

He would even get to see her brother on one of his return visits. They had been so close before Stephen died. This will be a grand surprise. And her parents, who had been so pleased with her choice for a husband! Although no great surprise as they always believed the two of them would end up together.

Bill will have his own guides to show him the way and to his parents, other family members, and to see all the things that Sarah and Felicia had shown her. He will have some down time before setting off to new and wondrous adventures. So they sat and drank their tea together, silently enjoying each other's company and listened to the music of the angels.

She marveled at his youthful appearance regained, after seeing him on the day of his transition. They both were the young couple of the early days of their marriage. Which made Christina realize that everyone she saw on this side of the veil was young and vibrant. "Why not," she thought, "this is who we really are!"

CHAPTER 45

Bill had been off with Benjamin and Frank, his two guides, enjoying all the visiting and adventures that Christina had experienced with Sarah and Felicia. He would come back to the cottage full of things to share with her.

"This is just like old times," Christina thought to herself, "sitting together and sharing the day's activities."
After she had heard his tales of Hath, Angela and Rafina, that were very similar to hers, she suggested they take another trip, together this time.

Bill agreed, anxious to see everything there was to see, reminding Christina of her impatience to see and do everything and NOW. She laughed and took his hand and told him just to let go.

He relaxed and felt himself being transported to somewhere. They both arrived in the room of Andy. He was busily doing schoolwork and stopped, looking up at the two of them.

"Granddad? Is that you?" Andy exclaimed. "And Steena!" The name he had become accustomed to calling her, not really knowing her as a Grandma.

Bill was amazed that Andy could see them both and answered him with great surprise in his voice, "Yeah, Andy, it IS me! It is wonderful to see you and even more so since you are able to see me and... Steena. Now you can let your parents know that we are doing fine and well and happy and together. Need some help with that homework?"

"No Granddad, I can do it myself! Besides you always told me not to cheat or copy in school because eventually I would get caught! Even if they can't see you and even know you were here, that still would be cheating, huh?"
"I am so proud of you, and yes, you are right. Steena brought me here to see you and tell you I am fine."

"I know, she comes here a lot and we talk, even play chess sometimes. Would you play chess with me sometime? Of course, you can't move the pieces, but you can tell me which ones to move, okay?"

"Andy, I would love to play chess with you. Next time I am here, just get that board out and I'll be happy to whip you at a game!"

"Oh, Granddad, you're still being funny."

Christina, smiled at Andy and said, "We are off to see your cousin next and give her the same message that we are fine."

"But Steena, we both already knew that!"

"I imagine you both did! We love you and we'll be back."

Andy waved at them and blew them both a kiss, "See ya soon!"

Steena took Bill's hand once again and they were off to Ashley's.

When they arrived, being an avid reader, Ashley was curled up in a chair reading a book, probably for the second time. They stood and watched her for a while and Christina could tell just by looking at her that she was a second very special and gifted grandchild. She had visited Ashley many times before and as Andy, she was able to see Christina from the very beginning and just accepted it as an every day occurrence. It was also helpful that their parents never contradicted them when they told of their visitations, but encouraged them to talk about it.

Feeling she was not along, Ashley looked up and exclaimed, "Granddad!" She jumped up from her chair and ran over to him wanting to give him a big hug, which, of course, she quickly discovered was not possible. "You just looked so real to me, I thought you were here!"

Acting offended, Bill replied, "I am real and I am here," then stuck out his lower lip in a pout.

"Oh, Granddad, you know what I meant! Hi Grandma! I'm glad to see you both together. This is my first time seeing you two together. How romantic!"

Christina rolled her eyes at Ashley and then leaned over and kissed Bill on the cheek, just to verify her belief in romance. Such an age!

"Okay, that's enough you guys. What are you doing here? Is everything all right?"

Bill answered her, "More than all right and that's why we are here. To let you know that. We are both wonderful, happy and still able to keep tabs on you kids, to keep you in line."

"Oh, Granddad, there you go again. Always teasing."

"Who said I was teasing? I just missed seeing your pretty face and dimpled smile, so here I am. Grandma missed you too! We will pop in from time to time to keep you and Andrew in practice seeing us. Give your parents our love and let them know all is well on the other side."

Laughing, Christina and Bill each blew kisses to Ashley and just shimmered away.

Back at the cottage, they both felt so privileged to have these children able to see them and hear them as though they were there in the flesh. They were determined to do this on a regular basis, to let them know they were very much alive and loved them very much.

"What a blessing they are. I sometimes wish I had been able to know them when I was physical, but this will definitely work for me."

Bill smiled at her and said, "Christina, they knew you so well, from Anne, Karen and me, that you may as well have been there for them. We kept your memory alive for both of them and we all talked about you frequently. They both also had your picture in their rooms. I wonder if that is one reason they are both so open to seeing you now."

"Whatever you all did for me, I love you for it. They are both so special and I believe they could be Indigo children."

Bill nodded in agreement and said, "The girls and I have discussed this before and have wondered the same thing. It seems they came into the world already knowing and their very presence makes people feel better."

Christina laughed, "Including me!"

CHAPTER 46

Many visits, chess games and book discussions later, Christina and Bill marveled at the way Andrew and Ashley had grown into beautiful, young adults. They were both very much a part of their grandchildren's lives. They shared in the joys and pains of their growing up. Plus it was easy to keep in touch with their daughters that way as well. Anne was able, to some degree visit with her Mother, just not as adeptly as her daughter.

Christina and Bill watched their grandchildren move through school with ease and then on to college. Their relationship was as strong as if they were on Earth with them. They both made friends easily and kept very busy with all the extra-curricular activities associated with college.

As is often the case, Ashley was so impressed with the help and care the family received for her grandfather, she decided to go into Social Work, then after getting her degree, she'd apply for a position with a hospice.

Andrew, a couple of years ahead of her, was aiming for a career in medical research. He often remarked there were a lot of years ahead of him so he was still trying to make that final decision of which direction to go.

Neither one of them had a deficit in the brains department and Christina and Bill knew that they would both be successful no matter what field they entered into.

Andrew's social life grew and he was at no loss for girlfriends, or at least dates. He was having fun along with his heavy workload. His motto seemed to be, "Must maintain balance in all areas." Even if it was a little lopsided at times in the girlfriend department. As time went on, one girl seemed to take up the majority of his free time. Melissa was definitely attracted to Andrew, a tall, athletic looking guy with bright blue eyes and light hair, who seemed to be the 'catch' on campus. Jock, he was not, but as popular as if he were. He just determined that sports were for watching, especially since he had so much on his plate. He did work out at the gym and enjoyed that, as it only took an hour a day and not a big chunk of his free time in practices and team meetings. Plus it gave him time to think.

Melissa was as dark-haired as Andrew was light. She also had the dark brown eyes to match. She was tall and slender and somewhat athletic looking. They made an impressive, striking couple and were beginning to be seen on campus together everywhere. Their relationship blossomed and grew and Melissa was loved by Andrew's family. Andrew was given full approval by Ashley, and she and Melissa became close friends. Melissa was a good fit for the family. Good thing, as it appeared that one day she was going to become part of the family.

Andrew became an intern at a local hospital, still trying to decide what area to go into, however, being pulled strongly by the research end of it.

Andrew had taken Melissa out to dinner and they went for a walk afterward down by the river where his grandparents so frequently walked.

Bill and Christina found themselves reminiscing over old times seeing the young couple possibly walking in their same footsteps. Bill was particularly drawn to Melissa and after pondering the connection, recognized her as his very close cousin with whom he had grown up in the same way that Andrew and Ashley had.

"Wow!" Bill said to Christina. "This can be mind-boggling sometimes. But fun!"

As they watched the young couple, they saw Andrew reach into his pocket and produce a small black box. He opened it, to one knee, and smiling at Melissa didn't say a word. She admired it and also didn't say a word. It somehow wasn't necessary. She leaned over and kissed him while helping him up at the same time and they embraced. Mid embrace, Andrew looked over Melissa's shoulder and saw Granddad and Steena admiring them both, nodding and smiling.

The next months were filled with work, wedding planning arrangements, with Melissa and Ashley doing most of the planning. Karen and Anne were busy trying to keep everything to a minimum and working closely with Melissa's Mother, who was in complete agreement with the 'minimum' part.

The wedding party had been selected, bridesmaids' dresses designed and made, ushers selected and everything was headed toward the big day.

The Big Day arrived. Nerves abounded. Andrew was ready. Melissa was ready. Ashley as one of the bridesmaids was ready. Music started. Bridesmaids walked down the aisle. Andrew stood with his groomsmen lending their support by his side.

Ashley was looking particularly beautiful that day in a dress the color of violets, which suited her perfectly. Her blonde hair was done up, giving her a look of elegance. Andrew gave her an approving look when she arrived. She also noted that Christina and Bill were there as well, off to the right of the altar, getting a good view of everything and in perfect view for Ashley. She nodded to Andrew who stole a quick look and saw them as well, and smiled. "Of course, they would be here," he thought to himself.

Next came the crowning moment and no single person was disappointed in the vision coming down the aisle at last. Melissa's dark hair and dark eyes stood out against the white, slender dress, looking for all the world like royalty. The epitome of elegance.

Andrew felt his breath catch and fleetingly wondered if he was going to breathe again.

As a special gift to the wedding couple Christina sent a white dove. The dove encircled the newlyweds as they left the church, descending the wide steps with their wedding party, and the guests erupted in multiple choruses exclaiming, "It's a sign of good luck," "What a beautiful co-incidence!" Of course Andrew and Ashley knew better.

During the ceremony, Ashley caught herself wonder-ing if any one of the guests could see Christina and Bill and she and Andrew did. "Probably not," she thought. Just as that thought floated from her mind, she saw Christina grin largely, place her hands on her heart and nod to one of the wedding guests. She turned in the direction of Christina's nod and saw a very handsome young man smile and with a twinkle in his eye, nod back. He then turned his eyes toward Ashley and his look made Ashley actually blush.

Unknown to Ashley at the time...not only was he a friend of Andrew's, but he was also a doctor!

CHAPTER 47

Sitting back in their cottage, with Bill relaxing in the wing-backed chair he loved so much in their Earthly home, Christina had the phrase ringing in her head, "like clusters of grapes."

"It is all so perfect and so beautiful and exciting. I almost can't wait to get back myself!" Christina exclaimed. Bill looked at her with a discerning frown on his face.

Christina caught the look and felt the immediate need to allay the concerns he may have about her leaving immediately. "No, no! Not yet. We still have lots to learn and see. Plus we have to wait for the right family as well, make choices, study our options. Stephen picked the ideal arrangement for his dreams to become a doctor and look where he is headed now!"

Bill relaxed back into his chair and dropped his hand to the side. He felt a very familiar nudge to his hand. He looked down and there was Tippy looking up at him and prodding him for a petting. It was as if he sensed Bill's concern and showed up just to provide some small comfort.

"I am just not ready to be separated from you again, that's all," Bill said, while scratching Tippy's ears. "Come here boy," he said and patted his thighs. Welcoming the invitation, Tippy jumped up into Bill's lap.

"Just think, Bill. We don't ever have to be separated again. In fact, we are not separate at all. Never have been and never will be. It has been the biggest insight and remembrance for me that we are all ONE and ONE with God. But being together again can be our choice or not our choice. Unless there is some unfinished business together that needs to be completed. But even then that choice is ours to complete the unfinished business. We can postpone the inevitable, but at some point we will have to face it and take the appropriate measures. I think that is absolutely amazing! We have made our choices in the past and will make them again, and again, and again. And right now, my choice is to be with you again, and again, and again."

Bill smiled at her and their colors blended into one beautiful glow filling their cottage with light. The love they had for each other was obviously never-ending.

"Have you given any thought to what you would like to do when you go back?" Christina asked.

"I guess I hadn't, but I will need to find out what my choices are. Have you?"

"I have thought about it, but no final decision yet. I supposed a lot will have to do with what we both decide, huh?"

Mid discussion the angel doorknocker sounded. Christina willed the door to open and usher in Sarah and Felicia. The three of them embraced and both girls headed for the window seat. Christina manifested two cups of tea and presented them to their dear friends.

"What brings you both to our tiny abode?" Christina asked.

Felicia spoke up first and looking at Sarah received a nod, "I'll start. I have finally decided that it is time for me to return to the physical. The family is there and, in fact, I have been in constant contact with the daughter. Please understand that what I am going to tell you is by mutual agreement. I was not thrilled with the idea of going through the early years and by the same token Victoria, that is the daughter's name, finished what she went there to do. This was also done with the understanding of the parents when they were on this side and making their Earth choices, although now it is not in their physical memory. A lot of agreement is involved when this is done, particularly on the part of the two participants. But, at a predetermined time, I will step in and take Victoria's body and she, having completed her Earthly goal, will come here. She will not, therefore, die and her family will not experience the loss. She is currently 16 years old. This has been blessed by all the 'powers that be.' I am being sent there to be a spiritual teacher at a critical time on Earth. I am not the only one and will be joined by others. Most of them have been there since birth. Mine is not a common situation, but one that can be used when necessary."

Christina had to consciously close her mouth and looked over at Bill who was having the same response. "Will we see you again?" She asked.

"Of course, I will be back to check in on you probably at night." Felicia then turned to Sarah, held out her arm with palm up with great flair as though introducing the next performance.

Sarah leaned back in the window seat and said, "Well, I'm staying."

"Thank goodness!" Christina started.

"But...I won't be here with you the same as before. You really don't need either one of us anymore to show you around and answer questions. You and Bill are now in a position to do for others, what we did for you. You may be assigned one or two new arrivals to escort and fulfill the roles we had. You might even decide to work with some of the people on the other levels we introduced you to and help them out of their self-imposed situations so they may move ahead into the beautiful.

"I am staying because I have chosen, and have worked for, the opportunity to train under the Masters. In time, after training, I will be a guide to someone in the physical, but in the meantime I will work and train with the Masters to help Mother Earth. As long as humans want to enter the spiritual path, we will help them; as long as humans want to clean up and heal Mother Earth, we will help them; as long as humans want to end the suffering, we will help them; as long as humans want to end the warring, we will help them.

We will do this by sending love, energy, beams of healing light, and yes, meditation. The Masters work for humanity on all levels. People in the physical have more help than they could ever imagine. When needed the Masters and Angels sometimes take human form to perform necessary tasks in order to save humanity from themselves. So, I will still be here and you both will see me when I am not studying and working and learning!"

Still in a state of shock, Christina jumped up and went to the window seat and hugged each of them, not knowing what to say. "One of the few times I am speechless. I am so happy for both of you. These are areas I had never considered before, but they both sound so exciting. I love you both and now maybe I have something else to strive for, and Bill too! We were just discussing our next plan of action!"
Sarah smiled and said, "We know, that's why we chose now to show up and tell you."

Christina was pondering everything they had been told. She turned to Felicia and asked, "Can anyone choose to stay here and not return to Earth?"

Felicia hesitated, collecting her thoughts and choosing her words carefully, "Many can. It is not for me to say who can and who cannot. It is all about love and the development of the ability to love unconditionally. When we have relationships on Earth, there is very often unfinished business and issues that are left unresolved. It is a give and take, action and reaction, the law of cause and effect, often described as karma. The idea of karma has gained a lot of popularity lately with the word being bantered about more frequently. Many of the eastern religions accept it as fact. The belief in karma generally instills the desire to do good rather than suffer the consequences. Just as a child would rather behave than face the ire of the parent. It is the idea of do no harm to another. It is also taught when we are very young as the Golden Rule, 'Do unto others as you would have them do unto you.'

"There may be debts imposed during a life on Earth and they may be owed you or you may owe a debt to someone else. It can be instant or it can be carried over to another, or even many other lifetimes with the affected person. These are checks and balances and an important part of learning unconditional love. Debts don't go unpaid. No good or bad deed goes unrewarded or unpunished. Through mutual agreement they can be done on Earth in the physical or here. There are so many sides to this it is very difficult to say who can and cannot stay here and choose not to return. Believe it or not, most souls choose to take a physical body again and again."

This was a lot of information for Christina and Bill to assimilate and they both just stared at each other with incredulous looks on their faces. Seeing this, another presence decided it was time to put in an appearance. The bouncing ball of light appeared in the corner of the room and it poured out the form of Josef.

"Please take this information and process it without forming any opinions. It will come to you naturally and you will fully understand it," Joseph said with his beatific smile that penetrated all in its presence.

"There are so many more possibilities that it will be extremely difficult for you to take them all in at this time. They go way beyond all human comprehension and it is all quite beautiful in its weave. These things will be made known to you at some point in your evolution, however, just to know it exists serves you well without having to understand all the details," Josef said as he waved his arms and covered the four in golden light. Each one felt the penetrating love and knowingness that all was well and in perfect order. With that, Josef just simply disappeared.

The four sat in silence for a while letting the feeling settle in and allowing themselves to bask in the glowing influence.

Thinking of her friends, Christina remembered hearing that the time for celebration should be at death more than birth and fully understood. Felicia was leaving home.

CHAPTER 48

In Earth-year time Christina and Bill watched their family for years to come. Anne and Karen aged, and they were there to meet Scott when he crossed over. For some time, Christina was by Karen's side, sending her love and support and strength. She longed to hold Karen in her arms and tell her it was all okay, as she did when she was a small child, and tell her that Scott was young, healthy and wonderful. However, in place of that she would send her signs of love that Karen picked up on. At times a bluebird visiting her at her kitchen window, and other occasions she would place coins at her feet in parking lots. These were easy enough for Christina to do now and Karen recognized where they were coming from. And this did provide her some comfort.

Scott adjusted quickly and was busy watching Andrew become a proficient medical researcher and scientist. Andrew and Melissa had two children, a girl and a boy, who were growing quickly.

Christina and Bill watched Anne and Ashley prepare for Ashley's wedding to the handsome doctor she met at Andrew's wedding. Christopher, (funny he had a name so similar to his sister Christina) and Ashley were working together in the hospice field; she as a social worker and he as a hospice medical director. Due to their professional lives they had children much later in their lives, a boy and then a girl.

Naturally, Christina just had to be there for the children of Andrew and Ashley. Andrew's daughter and Ashley's son, each the eldest, were also able to hear her and when they were very young she would read to them. However, they would hear more frequently than see her, but Christina still felt it was time well spent.

It is difficult to relate to time from the other side, due to the fact there really is no 'time line.' But pass it did, at least from the Earthly viewpoint.

After escorting, guiding and teaching many, many arrivals, often as a team, but more often as individuals, Christina and Bill were also being called upon to usher in their own beloved family. First there had been Scott, and eventually there was Anne, followed by Karen and lastly John. For each one they were at the bedside during ther final days and were side by side through the tunnel as they were greeted by other members of their families, friends and angels. Although they were all well into their years, each one returned to their youth once they reached the other side. In Earth time this took years, however, for Christina and Bill it happened almost without any lapse of time between arrivals. It was, as expected, a joyful, loving reunion welcoming them all home.

One of Christina and Bill's accomplishments was to help Felicia's Father, Mr. Nobody, move out of his desperation and into a place of more light. He was now with the Angel Angela. He was still not where Christina and Bill were, but he was in a much better place and had a thirst for knowledge and understanding. It would not be long. Felicia came back to see him when he was ready to accept her and they had a warm reunion. Christina and Bill went down to see him as well and continued to help him in every way possible. He and Bill would actually play chess and were establishing a friendship as good competitors with the usual laughter and back slapping.

They both provided a very warm welcome for all the newcomers to their level, but the most joyful moment of many, was to invite Maria, Walter and Gregory to their cottage when they arrived. Maria and Walter's two children Jeff and Harriet were the young adults they had worked hard to become.

Although they were enjoying their work, if you could really call it that, Christina began to feel another tug. A tug that she could neither deny nor ignore.

CHAPTER 49

After a very busy, yet fulfilling 'day,' Christina had been sitting on the floor of their cottage at Bill's feet as he sat in his favorite chair. She was resting her head on his knee. They had reached a point where speaking aloud was no longer necessary, but they were inclined to do it anyway. She looked up at him and her beautiful eyes still gave him pause, and had there been breath, it would have been taken away. He smiled at her and caressed her hair as he did in their days on Earth. He knew what she was thinking and also knew that there would be no putting it off. They nodded at each other and stood to take a walk together by their river.

Upon arrival at the river, they sat on the riverbank holding hands, each resisting voicing what was on their minds.

"It is time, isn't it?" Christina asked.

"I suppose it is. At times I feel it and at other times I find myself resisting it," he said as he studied the hand he was holding.

They looked out at the moving water and watched as two spheres seemed to drift on the currents and stop at their feet. One stopped before each of them and morphed into their two angels, Josef and Audrienne.

"We are here to help you both with important decisions. Not ones that have to be made, but we are here to offer options or even better, opportunities," the angels told them. "We could feel you both working this over in your minds, weighing the pros and cons for you at this moment, and we are prepared to offer you some entertainment!" Audrienne said. In unison, they said with flourish, "Presenting..."

With that word, the big screen that Christina had seen when her brother had visited, appeared across the river providing a perfect view.

Josef began, "Christina, there are a couple of options open for you. There are two different families you can enter into and each one has several avenues of opportunity or chance lines. In one setting you can have three different ultimate chance lines depending on your choices and the paths you decide to take. Those chance lines could lead you to a career as a writer, or you could become a concert pianist, or even an artist. In the best of circumstances you could possibly determine to become more than one of these."

As Josef cited these options Christina could view them on the big screen in front of them. Just a sampling... not in their entirety. She also noted that some of the pictures were slightly blurred.

"In the other setting, your choices could be quite different with one being a spiritual teacher, possibly with a church or organization, another could be lecturer/psychic on a very busy circuit with travel involved, and another could be a media personality with lots of public influence.

"The parents in both situations will be very supportive and the childhood and growing up will be loving and happy."

"Those are some difficult choices. Will Bill and I be together again?"

"This is a possibility. A reason we call them 'chance lines' is because of the free will of humans to make life choices. With your strong connection to one another and the fact that you have been together before, it is a strong likelihood that you would make that choice again. It will also depend on whether or not Bill chooses to return to the same time frame."

Bill quickly spoke up and said, "Wherever she goes, I go!"

At this juncture Audrienne spoke up and asked, "Bill, are you interested in seeing your choices at this time?" Almost afraid to say anything at all Bill just nodded.

"You also have some very interesting choices. You have both earned some very eventful and full lives for yourselves. Bill, you have one life with the chance of being a scientist, or an architect and a very successful one at that, or you could enter politics at a very interesting time in history. These are all in the United States, as are Christina's."

Viewing the screen, Bill was fascinated with his options, and began to ask questions, when Audrienne continued, "You have some other options in a different setting with a different set of parents. These parents are Christina's parents of before."

Christina found herself beginning to cry out, "Wait! They are my parents!" but caught herself realizing the ridiculous side of her 'old thinking.' However, not soon enough for Josef not to pick up on it.

Smiling at Christina Josef said, "You already knew that they are not your parents. You have all been together before and will again and again. No one belongs to any one else. In truth all souls are ONE, and we are all of God. Nothing and no one are separate. You might call it 'zero degrees of separation.' You have been brother and sister, cousin, mother and daughter and son, and it goes on and on. "Bill will have a beautiful relationship with them just as you did, should he choose this route. Bill, you can see here where you are an investor and quite successful, or you could go beyond to extend your last life's profession and be an archeologist, and there is also an opportunity for you to end up on the lecture circuit as well."

As he watched his potential futures on the big screen in front of him, Bill was feeling a little overwhelmed with all this information and asked, "Are we allowed to go to our cottage and think and talk this over, or is there a time limit here?"

Both Audrienne and Josef laughed at this, "Time limit? Are you already back in the physical? Take whatever you need to make your decisions. We will be here for you to answer any questions or to alleviate any concerns you may have. We will always be there for you as we have in the past, as we are while you are here, and we will be in your future. Like glue!" Joseph said.

Bill thanked them both and stood and hugged Christina. "We have a lot of thinking to do, not to mention decision making. So much to consider, so let's get to it."

Josef spoke up and said, "Please, before you go, permit us to clarify something for you. We have just outlined the strongest potentials for you both for your next physical life. However, nothing dictates that you must follow any one of these chance lines. Because it is your choice and because you have free will, you could conceivably choose to do nothing at all. Or, you could become a swim instructor, a waitress, a kindergarten teacher, a librarian, a landscaper, a trucker. The list goes on and on. And whatever you choose to do is okay. It is all for the experience. Do you get that?" Audrienne continued, "You also know that all memory of your time here and of your last lives will not remain with you. To remember, would serve you no purpose, and could possibly hinder decision making. Any memory that you may experience, could show itself as intuition, or a feeling of having done this before, or picking up a skill with great ease, because you had already mastered it in a previous life. All of this to your advantage, of course."

Christina and Bill nodded and they truly did understand. And all of it.

They both bowed slightly to Josef and Audrienne in thanks and received big smiles in return at which point the two angels became the spheres of golden-white light with the sound of small bells, and drifted away.

CHAPTER 50

Back at the cottage, Christina and Bill snuggled together on the over-stuffed couch. "A lot of choices we have to consider," she commented.

Bill was staring out the window and was slow to respond. "Yeah, I know," he said pensively.

"Are we rushing into this? Is this what we should be considering? Or is it just me pushing to go back? I must admit, I am feeling a tug to go back. How about you?" Christina asked.

"It is not just you. I feel this is what we should do and am okay with it. At moments I feel the tug as well. I guess this is what happens to most of us over here. Stay or go. Big decision. When? Another big decision. Which family? Another big decision. I must admit I am feeling a little overwhelmed at the moment."

"I feel confident that whatever we decide, we will be together again. I also realize there are some chance lines to follow to make it more apt to happen than others. So we will make this contract with each other that we will be together and that we will choose the right paths for each of us. How does that sound?"

"Sounds great to me!" With that Bill relaxed considerably, nearly all hesitation gone.

Both Bill and Christina spent time watching and observing the choices of families, developing a familiarity and an understanding of the life styles each would have to offer, along with the family dynamics involved. They would actually drift into the potential families' homes and spend time among them to get a better feel of the relationships, atmospheres and energies involved. They both knew this would aid them in making their final decisions of where they would best fit. After some study, Christina had pretty much decided on the family where she could best serve as a lecturer or media personality, or possibly something altogether different. She felt she "fit" with them the very best, physically, mentally, emotionally and spiritually. She also felt an already established relationship with them but couldn't put a finger on who or why.

Bill, on the other hand, was strongly leaning toward Christina's previous parents. He figured this would enhance the opportunity of being with Christina again, plus he had had such a wonderful relationship with them before with strong ties of love. He just loved what they had to offer and their spiritual strength was quite evident.

Back at their cottage sitting together once again, "Done!" Bill exclaimed. He was feeling as if he had accomplished some great feat.

Excited, Christina asked, "You have made your decision? You know where you are going?"

"Yup!"

"Well, smarty pants, so have I. What do you suppose we do now?"

"It seems sort of proper to tell Anne, Karen, Scott and John, don't you think? I'll invite them to join us." With that Bill sent out the message to their Earth children and they appeared at the cottage door. Just as Karen raised her hand to touch the knocker, Christina invited them in.

Christina began, "We thought you should be the first to know that we have decided to return to Earth and have made our decisions and chosen our families." She grinned in anticipation of the response they would receive.

Both girls rushed over and hugged their 'parents,' and became excited at the turn of events. They wanted to know everything, such as who, what, when and where.

Bill said, "We can't answer all your questions yet, and at this point, I guess we are waiting for some kind of direction."

With that the angel door knocker sounded. Silently Christina invited them in.

Josef stood before them in his angelic magnificence and said, "So you are wondering where you go from here? Judging by the party going on, you have made your decisions!"

Christina and Bill filled Josef in on the families they had chosen. Josef then gave them both additional information about their connections.

"Christina, you felt the connection to your new family, because they were your grandparents and now are Coralee and Kevin. They have been married 5 years and have one daughter who is three. That daughter was your cousin Emily. You will also have a younger brother a couple of years after your arrival."

Christina instantly remembered her short time with Emily. She and Emily were very close and lived within a bicycle ride from each other. They attended the same grade school and often tried to pass themselves off as sisters, which was pretty easy due to the similarity in looks. Emily was Christina's very first experience with the loss of a loved one, when Emily was diagnosed with leukemia and crossed over at the tender age of 12. Christina missed so much school as a result of Emily's death that she nearly flunked out of the 7th grade. He heart was broken and it took a great deal of love and caring from her parents to help her heal. Now here she was, getting another chance to be Emily's sister!

"This is unbelievably wonderful. Now we can finish what we started," Christina said with awe in her voice.

Josef continued, "Precisely! Your parents and Bill's parents are also close friends. They are considering it 'luck' that they are both pregnant at the same time. They are now Bethany and Jamison. Once again, it was no mistake that you chose the parents you did. Bill, your parents have been

married 3 years and you are their first born. They will have
two more children, a girl and then a boy.

"When the time is right, you will feel the unmistakable pull to your new life. Up to that point, you will still have
the opportunity to change your mind. You will also have the
opportunity to say your temporary farewells here and for a
short time you will be returning here with all memory, while
still in the infancy stages. Eventually you will become en-
meshed in your new life with memory of this life and your
previous physical life erased.

"So, now is your opportunity to go forth and enjoy
the time you have left here with your loved ones, knowing
that you will be together again!"

Christina added, "And again and again. Talk about
the cluster of grapes...."

"Exactly!"

Josef bowed to all the people in the room and with a
smile and a wink, left.

Christina and Bill grabbed each other a danced
around the room. Not wanting to be left out, the other two
couples did the same. It was truly a bon voyage party!

CHAPTER 51

Christina and Bill spent their remaining time visiting with old friends, their favorite places and returned to the different levels of existence to continue their work with the souls that thought they were stuck there. They also visited the halls of learning knowing there was still so much they didn't know. They walked among the crystal towers and buildings and absorbed as much as they could. They looked at them and felt them. They listened fully to the music in the air provided by the angels and to the lovely sounds made by the flowers and plant life. They touched them and took in their essences. They studied all the life around them in every aspect trying desperately to etch all the beauty and sounds into their whole beings so they would never ever forget.

"No wonder we have to keep coming and going over and over again. There is much that is impossible for the human mind to conceive and even from this viewpoint it is somewhat difficult. I go through periods of wanting to know everything! But at least now I know that it is all part of my own personal evolution and that it will come to me 'in time,'" Christina said to Bill.

As they walked around their familiar places, Bill had his arm around Christina's waist and she had her head leaning on his shoulder, a comforting position of their life together before. It was still somewhat daunting to think about going back and it brought up mixed feelings of joy and regret. Regret at leaving this wonderful and beautiful home, and joy at the new prospects of another exciting life together.

While they spent time together, occasionally they would feel that tug toward their new families. They would stop in and visit them and check the progress of the mothers and both were beginning to feel stronger and stronger connections to the parents, sometimes even causing them to stay longer than they initially planned. They were definitely easing into their new prospective lives.

One day while sitting along the banks of their created river, Christina felt the need to return to her new parents more strongly than before. She could almost feel herself being pulled away from Bill. Rather than fight it she gave into it and allowed it to carry her back to Earth. As she had suspected, her mother was going into labor. She watched as her father held Emily on his lap and at the same time held his wife's hand. She could feel the swelling of love for them imbed itself in her heart.

Returning to Bill's side, she said, "It is getting close and I will have to leave you." Grabbing his hand she begged, "Please reassure me that we will be together!"

Bill kissed her forehead and held her close and said, "We are connected now and forever. Remember, we will be back here together for a while before taking full possession."

Christina could feel herself being pulled and pulled. In spite of resisting it and reaching out her hand to Bill, she could see him becoming farther away, but still reaching his hand out to her.

In the delivery room her new father was still at his wife's side with Emily on his lap. Her mother was struggling and working hard at bringing Christina into the world. Then she heard the doctor exclaim, "It is a beautiful baby girl."

"Mommy, Mommy! My baby sister is crying!" Little Emily cried out. Both parents laughed at this and reassured her that her new little sister was just fine and she was just crying for joy.

As 'luck' would have it another mother was just admitted to the hospital and she and her husband were escorted to a labor room. While they were prepping his wife Bethany, Jamison left the room. He had heard that Coralee and Kevin had gone to the hospital hours ago and went to check on her progress. He received the news from the Nurse at the Nurse's Station that she had just moments ago delivered a little girl and the entire family was doing just fine.

Jamison was so excited that he rushed down the hall to Bethany's side and told her of the good news. They both laughed and cried and he kissed his wife who was about to go through the same thing as her best friend.

A short while later from an open door of the recovery room, Coralee saw the hospital staff wheel Bethany past the door to a nearby delivery room, followed by several people from their family. She smiled to herself.

Just as the recovery room nurse escorted Kevin in to be by Coralee's side, they both heard shouts of joy from across the hall, and above all the noise they distinctly heard the doctor's announcement, " It's a big , healthy boy!"

...And their stories and journeys begin...again.

ABOUT THE AUTHOR

Sandra Hatfield is a National Trainer with The Twilight Brigade Compassion in Action, a National training organization teaching people how to "be there" as a volunteer for the terminally ill and their families. She started as a Hospice Volunteer and then accepted a position as a Hospice Volunteer Coordinator. To date she has trained over 800 people in this field both with hospice and as a National Trainer. She is also a Certified Behavioral Therapist.

The subject of death has always held a fascination for her and she has done a lot of reading and research on the subject. Losing key members of her family at young ages is what led her to Dannion Brinkley's organization, The Twilight Brigade Compassion in Action and a lot of self-discovery.

Sandra has conducted an Angelic Connections workshop to help people get in touch with their personal angels as she does.

Sandra may be contacted at
angelconnection@windstream.net